Christmas in Hunter's Grove

*Forever Hanna
Series Book One*

K. M. MALAR

Stellium Books
Grant Park, Il 60940

May your days be filled with love + peace

*K.M. Mala
2018*

Cover Art by Annette Munnich
Photos Courtesy of the Author

All Rights Reserved
ISBN: 9781790587636
Manufactured in the USA
Stellium Books

DEDICATION

This book is dedicated to my children and grandchildren: Nicole, Andrew, Trey, Jesse, Emmy, and Riley. May you always believe in yourself, never giving up on your dreams.

TABLE OF CONTENTS

1. Once By Train   1
2. Feels Like Home   11
3. Comfort and Joy   29
4. Snowflakes from Heaven   49
5. In Sickness   65
6. Stay With Me   97
7. Camellias and Roses   127
8. Coincidence   139
9. If by Chance   155
10. Just Breathe   171
11. Crash   187
12. Second Chances   203
13. Enlighten Me   217
14. Don't Let Me Fall   237
15. Lost in the Moment   249
16. Open Handed   265
17. Six Words   285

About the Author   299

1
ONCE BY TRAIN

When a person feels they have only three choices which are fight, flight or freeze, mentally and physically their body is under such extreme stress that the emotional and physical pain leaves them debilitated. Hanna was such a person. It had ruined any relationship she had ever had, leaving her feeling toxic and poisonous to anyone who ever chose to love her. Being alone this holiday season was exactly what she had needed, but plans had changed, and she would soon find herself traveling back to her hometown.

Hanna had taken her medication just before her long journey back east for the holidays. Stepping onto the train, she heard the conductor yell, "All Aboard!" Upon boarding, she glanced down the aisle before finding the perfect window seat at the end of the car. Hanna's boots came off and slippers placed upon her petite feet, her coat unbuttoned with a pink velvety faux fur blanket that she pulled out from her carry-on. Hanna reclined her seat tucking the blanket in and around her as her mother did every night as a little girl. Her cell phone was placed on charge, carefully situated between her and the window.

Hanna had her scarf in her right hand and her left was tightly wound around her prescription bottle. Still uncomfortable she had placed her scarf under her head, using it as a makeshift pillow. She made herself as snug as possible as she closed her eyes for the long journey. As calmness had taken over her being, within a moment the conductor had come upon Hanna's seat slowly asking to see her boarding pass. Hanna immediately went into a whirlwind. Forgetting about showing her ticket, she was frantically scrambling through her purse to find it. The conductor leaned down asking Hanna if she was ok, she just looked up at him with tears in her eyes and a smile. He noticed the pill bottle in her hand and questioned if there was anything he could do. Hanna looked up once again to see the heartfelt look on the man's face. He was an older gentleman, mid-sixties, tall, mustache, rugged good looks, and strong southern voice. He was what most would think of being a true country boy who had worked on a farm his whole life. His eyes were comforting and seemed to have a genuine soul, someone that Hanna immediately felt safe around. She explained her situation to the stranger, on the verge of hyperventilating when he sat down beside her.

The whistling sound of the train's horn sounded as a sorrowful call on this bitterly cold night. But, Hanna was focusing on the rumbling melody where the wheels and steel met, with its increasingly chugging sound as the train made its way down the track, clickety clack, clickety clack. She went on to explain to the gentleman why she had chosen this means of travel, due to her high anxiety and claustrophobia. "A plane, I would never make it," she explained. Hanna's way of thinking was that when the train made stops, if she needed fresh air she would walk to the door, she knew her feet were on the ground so to speak and had emergency scenarios not only in her head but in a tablet as well, just in case she would fall in need of it. She never traveled anywhere without knowing there was a way out, a way in and a hospital or lifeline of some sort within reach. Her panic attacks had consumed her for over eight years, causing her to miss out on so much of life. This journey, although expected, was not welcoming. The conductor held her hand, told her he would keep an eye on her throughout her adventure and he would see to it himself that she kept safe. Hanna with a soothing look on her face, and anxiety gone from the joints of her body smiled, relaxed and for the first time in what seemed forever enjoyed the ride.

Hanna had been on her journey for six hours, peacefully sleeping when the engineer came over the intercom with a weather message. "ATTENTION PASSENGERS, we're sorry to announce that the 6:19 Northern service to BWI will be delayed. This is due to a winter storm that has taken a northwestern path straight towards us that will collide with a much larger storm that's dropping in the direction of our path as well. We are taking an alternate route and have received permission ahead that we will be stopping in Hunter's Grove Ohio. This is not an original stop, so we will have cab services available and vouchers for local accommodations. We are sorry for the delay this may cause to your journey. Further information is available from the station's mobile site, we will transport from our arrival point on forward as the weather permits."

The conductor immediately thought of Hanna one car behind and promptly made his way to her side. Hanna, making out pretty much all the information the engineer had shared was a little confused and very anxious. Her head was pounding, the fear of not knowing what could happen in the storm had her anxiety crawling up her spine in a frenzy. Within seconds Hanna's vision started spinning, passing out from hyperventilation. "Hanna," the conductor said with his soft yet rugged voice while patting the sides of her face. "Wake up ladybug, come on, wake up." A few moments went by before Hanna regained consciousness. "All right how are we doing now?" He was holding Hanna's face with both hands, looking into her emerald green eyes. Hanna's body had gone into an overwhelming panic attack. She was dazed, sweat pouring off her body, her heart rate felt as if it had tripled and her palms and feet felt frozen.

She replied fearfully, "What am I going to do? Where am I going to go? I don't know where I am." The conductor sat down once again beside her, taking her by the hand. At this point, he realized it was time for a proper introduction to the sweet green-eyed girl. An introduction that would put her at ease and erase the panic that was filling her body at that very moment. "Hanna, my name is Pete, I was a medic in the United States Marines for twelve years, which four of those were in the war. I've been on these trains for close to twenty-three years, trust me we have emergency plans in place on this train, first aid kit, the works." Pete trying to gain Hanna's trust, "The town that we're headed to has a hospital and did I mention that I'm great under stress? You're safe, I promise."

As he gave her a calming smile Pete noticed the prescription bottle in Hanna's hand, he pried it from her grip, saw what it was for and asked her how many she had taken within the past 24-hours. Hanna looked up at him expressing with the rise of a finger that she had only had one. She took the bottle from Pete's hand, opened it and placed one of the tiny pills under her tongue. He took her hand once again to help calm her. "Ladybug, we look to be stuck here for at least two to three days. No flights, bus or train services will be running, however, we are only ten minutes, fifteen tops from our destination that we will call home for the next couple of days. I assure you that everything is going to be fine." Pete let Hanna know he would take care of all the arrangements for the two of them as far as food and a warm place to stay. His next worry was finding a way to refill any medications she may need before the storms collided. He took her blanket and gently pulled it up close to her chin. "Now, take a few deep breaths, unwind and I'll be back soon. I just need to go take care of the other passengers, and again don't worry, I'm right here." Pete had quickly become Hanna's angel of comfort, it was his strong masculine voice that gained Hanna's attention each time he spoke a word. Although rough, it gave Hanna the security that he was in control and everything was fine.

As the train tiptoed closer to Hunters Grove it started making an awkward rumbling sound, the howls of the whistles, the hissing and screeching from the breaks. Hanna looked out the window to see the snow was falling fiercely. She felt they were decelerating but the snow itself, seemed as if they were still traveling faster than what she felt they should be. Something was off, she knew they were reducing speed, so she thought, but something just felt out of the ordinary. Pete stopped back to Hanna to let her know he would be getting the other passengers off and into cabs. He also made a quick remark that he had rooms reserved for them at a quaint Inn for the next couple of nights. Hanna kept her blanket up close to her, staring out of the window and awaited Pete's return. "Pete," Hanna expressed boisterously.

"Are you ready for an adventure?" Pete asked with a smile. "Come on, I have your bags and a cab waiting just on the other side of the station. Hanna quickly took off her slippers placing her boots back on. She tucked the slippers away in her carry-on bag, keeping her blanket out to fight off the frigid temps that lurked outside the doors. She packed her phone, placed her purse upon her shoulder, covered herself with her blanket and held on tight to her medication and carry-on.

Pete extended his hand, Hanna laying hers into his as he helped her off the train and into the unfriendly night air. The snow was whipping with strength, hitting Hanna hard. Any anxiety that was left running through her body had dissipated in an instant, for she felt her body go into a mild shock. Placing her blanket up around her face, Hanna reached for her gloves that were tucked deep into her coat pockets. Pete, being her only light of hope on this trip started explaining to her the history of the old station. The way he saw it, the more he kept her mind occupied the less time she had to have a relapse into another attack. "I know this is scary and you've never experienced anything like this before but don't worry ladybug, I, unfortunately, have in my railroad years and guess what? Everything turned out just fine. Now look here, this building was constructed in 1907, this station has a twin ya know, she was built in Washington Indiana. But this old girl, she's been closed for a great deal of time now. Trains still pass by and I'm sure the neighborhood kids and some of the ole timers catch a wave occasionally from the engineers, but only memories remain." Hanna glanced over to see a memorial that had been placed outside of the station back in 1926 by the Daughters of the American Revolution. It marked the beginning of Hunters Grove as it stands now. Listening to Pete's story her eyes wondered over to Willows Creek, she imagined the earlier days where life was simple yet hard. Steamboats traveling down the murky waters, the hundreds of people who must have waited in her exact spot for shipments of much needed items to survive, mail and family members from the train. By now she was freezing, Pete had loaded her luggage into the trunk of the cab and Hanna welcomed the warmth that flowed out the back door as Pete opened it for her.

Christmas in Hunter's Grove

2
FEELS LIKE HOME

As they made their way down Main Street, Hanna was mesmerized by the falling snow. It sparkled against the Christmas lights like glistening diamonds that streamed across the road. The snow embellished the Christmas trees and stars dangling from lamp posts. All the stores were of the past with the soft glow of twinkle lights in every window front with the most creative Christmas displays. She saw the most exquisite mannequins dressed in 1800's apparel on every street corner, from the bonnets and top hats to the shoes they wore. Pete leaned over to Hanna, "So what do you think? You're getting to see firsthand Dickens Victorian Village, one of the most magical towns in history this time of year." Hanna's eyes moved with excitement from one side of the street to the other, taking in the beauty and magic that she had never had the privilege of witnessing before.

"Wait, you said Dickens? From one of my favorite Christmas books, Dickens?" Pete nodded his head, tipping his hat with a smile upon his face and a twinkle in his eye.

With what Pete would call a hop, skip and jump down the road they arrived at The Colonel's Inn. It was a glorious Queen Anne style mansion where the snow-covered roof pitches flowed into one another. There must have been over eight with what she was seeing. The architecture was very early 19th century with a front-facing gable; overhanging eaves; a glorious porch covering part of the front facade, including the front entrance columns with bay windows along with multiple chimneys. The colors appeared to be made up of brick and tans. The Spindles were of black and cream with the greatest attention to detail. The cab driver pulled up exiting the vehicle to gather Hanna's luggage from the trunk. Pete kindly paid the driver and grabbed most of her baggage himself, except for her carry-on that was still glued to her side. Making their way to the front door Hanna quietly turned to Pete, "Thank you." Pete smiled as he opened the door where they were greeted with the warmth and luminosity of the fireplace.

It was now well into the early morning hours, room keys were laying upon the check-in counter with a note that read:

"Greetings,
Please make yourself comfortable for the night.
I will welcome you properly in the morning.
P.S. I will have a late breakfast for you in the
dining room around ten, you have had a long
trip and need your rest,"
Sam

Hanna and Pete followed the glow from the lanterns up the staircase to the first floor with Pete dropping Hanna's luggage to the Lilac room before retiring for the night himself. Hanna was extremely drained from a mixture of excitement and her medication that she immediately laid upon the bed. Within just a few moments she heard footsteps plodding up the stairs. Thinking Pete may have forgotten something she called out for him. "Pete, can you come here for a moment?" No answer was ever returned. An overwhelming feeling of the unknown sent chills through Hanna's body. There was a hint of a sweet aromatic smell from pipe tobacco that appeared to stream in from beneath the door.

Although not seen, an angelic vibration floated within the room as to say, "Sleep well, my child." Still dressed and holding on to her blanket, Hanna within moments had drifted off into an enchanted sleep.

Pete woke around nine, his morning routine always consisted of light exercise, a hot shower, and grooming for the day ahead. He was sure to place his clothes from the night before in the laundry bag and made his bed before prancing his way downstairs to the dining hall to meet Sam. "You must be Pete," a welcoming hand leaned out to shake his. "Wasn't sure if you all were going to make it, but glad you're here safe and sound, sit, please." Enjoying a remarkable sausage egg casserole. They engaged in quiet conversation when Pete started explaining the situation that had occurred the day before, how he met Hanna and how he could not bear to leave her fending for herself over the next couple of days. Pete went on to explain that It had been eight years since Hanna had to travel alone since being hit with what doctors confirmed as PTSD along with other mental illnesses.

"Hanna struggles daily on the inside to keep one foot in front of the other. Most days, she's good at hiding it from the world, however other days are much worse for her." Pete leaned back in his chair upon taking his last bite. "She's in her mid-thirties, green eyes, welcoming smile and a beautiful heart."

Sam interrupting, "About the mental illness part Pete, are we talking something I need to be concerned about while she's here? As in being a disruption to guests who may arrive?" Sam asking with an edgy look before taking a sip of his coffee.

"Oh no, no" Pete shaking his head with a slight laugh to his voice, "Were talking anxiety and panic attack issues, afraid to be by herself, afraid of the unknown and what may kill her is more like it. Harmful to herself or anyone else, causing disruption? No way, there is so much life in those eyes that is just screaming to be released." Sam listening quietly as Pete spoke of Hanna, you would have thought he had known her for a lifetime. What an impression this young lady had made upon him.

"She must be something special," Sam spoke to Pete.

"Oh, just you wait, she's a butterfly who wrapped herself back up into her protective cocoon."

"What is that supposed to mean?" Sam, looking for a pen and envelope. Pete took another sip of his coffee,

"It means until you break through that outer layer of hers, you will never know the real Hanna, nor will I. You can tell she wants to be a part of this world again so desperately, but afraid to take the steps to be able to get there."

"And you learned all of this within a couple of hours on a train?" Sam turning towards Pete as he sat down to write her a note.

"I've lived a long time, I can read people pretty quickly, able to see the real person behind the eyes, just wait, you will see firsthand what I'm talking about." Pete got up from the table to refill his coffee along with grabbing a warm muffin from the basket. "I'm going to head up to the room to make a few calls concerning the storm, if you need any help just holler, you know where to find me". Pete slipped quietly up the stairs as Sam was still sitting at the table writing.

Hanna woke to the sound of a quiet knock at the door where she noticed an envelope laying on the floor. As she sat up, feeling a bit disoriented upon opening her eyes she remembered being so cold with an awful headache. But she smiled as she remembered the beauty of the Christmas lights that had been bestowed upon her eyes. Hanna noticed she was still in her clothes from the night before as she stumbled from the bed. Brushing the chill from her arms, she picked up the letter to open it.

Good Morning Hanna,

I hear you had a pretty exciting journey so far after talking to Pete this morning. I know you must be exhausted so don't worry, I'll bring you up some breakfast around eleven. It will give you some time to gather yourself. Oh, I also know new surroundings aren't your cup of tea but know your safe and the Lilac room is yours until your journey continues.
Look forward to meeting you
Sam

The menu for the next couple of days was enclosed with the letter. Hanna looking over all the scrumptious items made her realize just how famished she was. Apple French toast, Egg and Sausage casserole, Canadian bacon with sour cream coffee cake, the items were endless. Marking off what she was eager to try with a side of orange juice, her favorite, she quickly tucked the paper back into the envelope and slipped it under the door. Hanna stood there for a moment wondering if that's what she was to do, she knelt to look under the door where she saw a pair of men's shoes walking away. Never meeting the Innkeeper, she had no idea who left her the note, much less who would be serving it and how many people worked in such a large place. Sam, who's' shoes Hanna had obviously seen had been waiting on the other side of the door to see if she would get his letter or if he would just surprise her over the next couple of days with a breakfast made especially for her. She jumped to her feet, looked at her watch and scrambled her way to the bathroom to see how frightful she must look after the past few hours. Fighting with her anxiety and still a tremendous headache she tried her hardest to focus on the task at hand, getting ready for a new day.

Hanna took some time to get herself presentable, she was not expecting to be at a lavish bed and breakfast in the middle of nowhere, her thoughts where she would be with her parents by now. "Parents, oh crap!" Hanna quickly looking for her phone, forgetting she had plugged it was sitting on the nightstand where she grabbed it to see four missed calls from her mother. She dialed her mom immediately explaining what was taking place and that she was ok. They spoke for a brief few minutes before Hanna explained that she needed to finish getting ready and would call soon. However, her mother wasn't quite finished, wanting to know why she waited so long to travel, how the holidays were going to be ruined and she should have paid more attention to the weather. Hanna sat down on the bed, phone in one hand and her head in the other, as she knew somehow this would be all her fault. Before hanging up, Hanna apologized, let her mother know she could have never known this was going to happen and that she loved her.

A knock at the door startled Hanna as she was looking for another outlet to charge her computer. With makeup on, her hair still in a towel and instead of clothes, a long white plush robe, compliments of the Inn wrapped her skin. She opened the door expecting the maid, instead, a beautiful man stood before her. He was rugged with a well-kept beard, gorgeous plump lips, and humble blue eyes. He was husky built with broad shoulders, yet muscular and well preserved. "Um, good morning," Hanna managed to speak after standing there for what seemed a lifetime staring at this strange man.

"Good Morning Hanna, I'm Sam," as he entered the room, crossing Hanna's path to the opposite side of the room with a beautiful tray of food that was sat perfectly on the table. "I hope you slept well, I know it was not probably a lot, but hope it was enough to get you started for the day."

Hanna turned to address Sam, thoughts flowing in her head, well dressed, polite, down-to-earth. "Um yes, I slept well, I think I may have fallen asleep as soon as I laid down, keeping the strange occurrences to herself. "Sam's breakfast smells like heaven right about now." Her eyes wandering around the room for the first time since arriving, grasping the robe wrapped tightly around her. "This room is glorious, I've never seen anything quite like it," She took notice of The Lilac Room, which was located down a private hall with its delicate lightly colored sage walls, and a complete wall of lilacs in the bath. Deeper shades of sage, pink and lavender filled the room. The charming sitting area that placed two wing backed chairs in a stunning bay window, the fine antiques including lighting, armoire and a hand-carved queen four poster bed all but completed the room. But the fireplace was certainly a striking warm welcome, for Hanna had not tried to work it yet, but it was certainly inviting.

"My mom always did the decorating for all of the rooms, my dad just oversaw the heavy lifting and construction," he chuckled lightly, looking around the room. "Here, you must be cold, I don't think the temperature outside has even hit into the teens yet today." He walked over by the bed and brought out a pair of white plush slippers that matched her robe and took the remote from the bed's side table turning on the fireplace. "This will warm things up for you." Hanna smiled with an overwhelming feeling in the pit of her stomach, nothing she had ever felt before and not even sure how to describe it, but she was happy, excited, comfortable. "Well, I'll let you be for now, if you need anything you can find me down in the gathering room straightening up some." Sam excused himself from the room, leaving Hanna alone to enjoy her breakfast and to finish getting ready.

Hanna took a moment and sat down in one of the mauve winged back chairs, soaking up the warmth of the fireplace while looking contently out at the brutal snowfall. The breakfast that Sam prepared was absolutely to die for and not only did he bring her orange juice but hot chocolate in a ceramic pale blue coffee mug with a matching topper. She sat in peace sipping her hot beverage still gazing out the window. The trees even though heavy with snow, glistened. The yard made up of juniper, spruce and pine were almost completely covered. Everything was bright and electrified. The fireplace set the mood in Hanna's room. Cozy, snug and warm, she was exactly where she was supposed to be during this violent weather. Hanna took her time, enjoying a homemade breakfast. The smile that came upon seeing Sam for the first time had not left her face. She was at peace and relaxed. Upon finishing the last bite of the coffee cake, she made her way into the bathroom. Hanna didn't exactly want to come across as a hermit in her room, after all last night's festivities including the pipe smell she wanted to spend as much time as she could by studying the Inn and Sam.

Upon getting dressed Hanna went out to the nightstand where her watch, prescription and phone lay. She was dressed in a pair of cream leggings and undershirt along with a flannel in hues of pinks, cream and black that hung loosely over her. She leaned over to zip up her boots before placing her room key and phone in her pocket, her prescription bottle was slid into the side of her boot, not to be noticed. Sliding her watch on she placed her dirty clothes in a linen bag, gathered her dishes, dimed the lights and walked out of her room closing the door every so lightly to not wake any possible guests.

Sipping on her hot chocolate she found her way down the luxurious staircase that ended in the grand entryway. The walls were white with spiced oak wainscot, distressed oak floors and oak trim. With twelve-foot ceilings, she noticed one of the largest Christmas Trees she had ever laid her eyes upon standing strong in front of her. Decorated in what appeared to be past family glass ornaments mixed with replicas of the 1800's it was a magnificent piece of art. She focused on this moment before entering the gathering room. The same architecture and motif shadowed into the spacious room. It's where during the Victorian era people and families would gather in front of the fireplace. Not only did it provide the necessary heat for warmth and cooking, it was thought to add a snug, warm atmosphere to the room as well. They were so right, it was perfect. Another large Christmas tree stood diagonally of the fireplace. Décor complimenting the striking foyer, except this tree was filled with glass Santa Claus ornaments of different time periods, pinecones and strings of popcorn. Atop was the most gracious angel looking down with praying hands, she wore a red velvet dress with white feathered wings, her face made of porcelain. Perfect in every way, Hanna could not believe the emotions that had taken over her body. The room fully decorated for Christmas with swags of greenery that moved from the gathering room to the grand foyer and up the staircase. The greenery and twinkle lights showered over doorways, fireplace mantels, over mirrors and wrapped oh so perfectly around the doorway to the Inn. Incorporated in the greenery were blossoms of red poinsettia. Hanna was experiencing Christmas as she had always dreamt of.

Sam was carefully hanging the last wreath in the bay window. For a moment, Hanna sat quietly in front of the masterpiece of the roaring fire watching Sam as the flames danced to their own melody. She could not believe that not even twenty-four hours ago, she was so stressed and what felt to be on the verge of a nervous breakdown. Not one thought of taking her medications had crossed her mind all morning, however, the headache was still evident along with a chill to her bones that she could not shake. "Pete!' Hanna was happy to see her new friend as he walked into the room, "Here, come sit with me." Pete moved slowly with his head halfway down towards Hanna perching on the corner of the sofa. "Pete, what's wrong? You look uneasy."

Sam turned around with concern as he walked over to them both. Pete turned to Hanna with a slight smile on his face. "Hanna, how are you enjoying your stay? Is it anything like you thought it would be so far?"

Hanna looked at him with a perplexed look on her face, "Really Pete," she said with a slight smile, "Are you trying to prepare me for bad news?" Pete had been speaking to Sam over the past couple of hours while Hanna was getting ready, it looked as if Sam's guests would not be making it to the Inn over the next few days and that Hanna and Pete were going to be staying put for a few more as well. "The storm, although it has stopped snowing is far from over. It stalled just northeast of us dropping over an extra foot of snow in areas of travel. We are looking to get an additional foot or more here as well." Hanna gazed at him with mild concern, hands locked together, shoulders tensed "So we would be staying here?" Hanna said with a calm voice.

"Yes," Sam spoke up. If you need to get any prescriptions refilled or need anything from the store Pete and I are making a run into town, we want to be sure we have enough food, candles and gas for the generator to keep things going over the next few days. You may also want to call your mom, give her the phone number here as well just in case we lose cell service." The look upon Hanna's face went from a slight smile to an anxious, glare.

"Hanna, please don't worry, I can show you how close the hospital is in case of an emergency if that would make you feel better and while you're here, think of this as your home."

Pete rose from the corner of the sofa, "This is the first Christmas without his parents here to decorate for the upcoming festivities, his employees were due to be at work this week after spending time away with their own families' gatherings and then... well... with the weather, it's just him." Hanna looked up at Pete with an uneasiness in her eyes.

"Hanna," Sam sparking her interest towards something else. "Let's get ourselves together first and get our running done, I have a four-wheel drive parked out back, so no worries there. Most of the stores are shut down outside of town, however the shop owners off Main Street, most of them live in loft apartments above their stores. There is a pharmacy just a few doors down where we will pick up some groceries, what do you say, go with us?" Hanna immediately took her phone from her pocket and dialed her mother. Giving her all the details of the upcoming storm, that she was safe and went on to tell her mother that she was excited to be a part of all of it. She was in the most stunning Christmas town, just down the street from the county hospital and that her accommodations at the Inn were exquisite. Hanna went on to calm her mother stating the abundance of food, warmth and friends were more than enough to keep her safe and out of harm's way. After a few moments, she hung up with another I love you.

Hanna turned to Pete, "Are we ready?"

Pete smiled, "Good girl."

It was after 3:00 pm, Hanna rushed up the stairs to collect her purse, coat, gloves. She was a little OCD, always knowing precisely what she needed and when she needed it. Sam and Pete were sitting in conversation by the fire when Hanna returned eagerly to the gathering room. "Well I think I have everything I need, I hope it's not colder than what it was last night or I'm going to freeze." "Crap," Hanna blurted out, running back up the stairs to get her pink blanket, she never traveled without it, it kept her calm, focused.

"Should we tell her there's an elevator?" Sam snickering as he walked towards the fireplace.

"Not yet, I think the extra exercise will help her anxiety. I know it would mine." Both gentlemen laughing in conversation as Hanna ran back down the stairs slightly out of breath to see the two men standing before her.

"Are we ok now?" expressed Sam, still smiling. Hanna just stood there with her head tilted to the side looking at Sam. Pete laughing,

"I see our butterfly is coming out of her cocoon." Shaking his head while walking towards the door.

3
COMFORT AND JOY

Sam had already started the truck to let it warm. Hanna, perkier than usual had a glow in her eyes. "Are we ready everyone, seat belts buckled, little missy?" Sam notable flirting with Hanna as he looked in the rear-view mirror.

Pete observed Sam's body language as he and Sam exchanged eye contact. "Sure, let's get going, daylight's a wasting," Hanna responding. The two men laughed, rolling their eyes. A little fresh air was going to be good everyone, not knowing when they would be able to get out again. Sam took the long way into town allowing Hanna some time to just breathe.

Hanna more than anyone was enjoying the short ride. She found herself stretching out instead of the dreaded feeling of being closed in like back on the train. Taking their time to drive the short distance into town, Hanna was happy to see the county road services, however, she became struck with fear as the roads were in awful shape. All she could think about was if she were to get sick or injured, would anyone be able to get to her. With the upcoming storm approaching and all the snow that had already fallen her anxiety started to hit a little hard. The mounds of snow were impressive and she began to take on the reality of it all. Looking down at the prescription bottle in her hand, she fought not to open it.

"Sam, can we be sure to stop at the pharmacy during our shopping trip?" Hanna asked in a calm voice, refocusing her eyes taking in the beautiful scenery of the snow above the mountain peaks that lay in front of her.

"Sure, but we need to be sure to stop and check on Mr. and Mrs. Whittle first."

"Who?" Hanna with a perplexed look on her face.

"Mr. and Mrs. Whittle, they have been like family to me after mom and dad passed. They don't have much and are barely making a living any longer

30

with their craft store up on Main." Hanna got quiet, she knew what it felt like to lose a parent, but no idea the feeling with both gone. She barely knew anything about Sam except that he seemed to have a big heart. In and out of the stores they roamed, picking up enough groceries to feed the town it seemed. Toiletries, a couple bottles of wine, gas for the generator and Hanna's prescription. He even stocked up on the necessities for his first aid kit along with enough ingredients to bake for what seemed a year.

"Do you think we have enough stuff?" Hanna giggled lightly. Sam looked in the rear-view mirror, noticing how magical her eyes seemed to gleam every time she smiled.

"Well, that depends, how much do you eat?"

Hanna got that crinkle on her nose and between her eyes, "Well that depends on how well you cook!" She fired back with a sarcastic look on her face.

"Mr. Whittle, what is he doing shoveling his front walk?" Sam quickly pulled up in front of the store where he and Pete jumped out of the truck. "Stay in here and keep warm, I won't be long, promise," Pete closing the door to the truck. A conversation was taking place between Sam and Mr. Whittle it seemed while Pete was finishing the front walk. Sam came back to the truck, "Hanna, do you think we could put groceries on yours and Pete's lap, would you mind?"

"Sure, do you want me to rock them to sleep while I'm at it?" Hanna with her witty humor.

Sam let out a slight laugh, shaking his head, "No my dear, Mrs. Whittle has been under the weather, Mr. Whittle has been trying to keep everything running smoothly but they don't have nearly enough supplies if the power fails and Mrs. Whittle needs to stay as warm as possible. I'm bringing them back to the Inn with us once Mr. Whittle goes in and packs up some of their belongings." Hanna smiled back at Sam, without a word, starting repacking the groceries that were in the back seat, placing a few bags in the front of the truck for Pete to hold onto and making enough room for all five of them to fit comfortably.

Hanna watched as Pete helped Mrs. Whittle out of the store and onto the sidewalk. Her back was extremely hunched over as if all the worries of the world had at one time weighed down upon on her shoulders. She was petite and frail, her silver hair although thinning, was medium in length and wavy, yet well-manicured. Her skin, though wrinkled, kept a beautiful rose undertone and her blue eyes held strength and wisdom. Mr. Whittle seemed to be in better shape, he was around six-foot-tall, mostly bald, thin looking but not undernourished. You could tell that maybe back in the day he played football or was a part of the military like Pete had been. He held onto the other side of Mrs. Whittle as they carefully walked to the truck, Sam had a small set of wooden steps in his hand, along with their luggage.

"What in the world?" Hanna immediately thought to herself until the back door opened, Sam placing the steps up on the sidewalk where they were able to help Mrs. Whittle walk up into the truck. Then following behind was Mr. Whittle. "Hello dear," exclaimed Mrs. Whittle, I'm Amelia Whittle, it looks like we are going to be spending some time together during God's glorious play."

Hanna smiled back at her, "Yes, yes we are, you have a beautiful town here Mrs. Whittle," Mrs. Whittle sat quietly smiling, not hearing a word that Hanna had spoken.

The ride was quiet back to the Inn, Hanna just stared out the window at the everlasting snow and the amazing lights dancing amongst it. The sun was almost set and the darker it got the more Hanna was just taking it all in, she felt so alive. She was excited at how perfect the snow seemed to fit in with the town's displays. She was amazed and relieved at the same time to see so many townspeople amongst the snowy streets. It calmed her knowing that the five that sat in the truck were not the only ones in town. She knew better, she knew there were over 100 other passengers' including the engineer from the train that were nestled between the two hotels just down the street. None the less, seeing with her own eyes helped her anxiety stay in check.

They returned to the Inn as darkness covered the night sky. The snow had begun to fall once again, the wind picking up and temperatures dropping swiftly. Pete and Sam quickly got Mr. and Mrs. Whittle out of the truck, walking them to the back door. Hanna grabbed their two luggage bags and was right on their heels. Upon entering the kitchen area, they sat Mr. and Mrs. Whittle down at the small oak dining table allowing them to catch their breath and warm the cold from their bodies. Sam asked Hanna if she would take their belongings just down the back hall to the last room on the left. With kindness in her eyes, she shook her head in agreement and made her way down the short hall. Sam put a pot of hot water on the stove for tea and filled the coffee maker. Pete walked quietly back out to the truck to gather the groceries and Mrs. Whittle's steps.

Entering the majestic bedroom, Hanna sat down the luggage to find the light switch. As the room lit up she could not believe what stood before her eyes. Already decorated for Christmas with the grandest pieces. If she didn't know any better, she would have sworn she was in the middle of a dream. "Good Lord, Santa himself must live here." The light switch controlled not the lamp but the snow-covered Christmas Tree that sat between the fireplace and sitting area. It was decorated with twigs, cardinals nestled inside of nests, red berries, yellow rose buds and poinsettia blossoms, red sheer plaid ribbon entwined within the branches and the lights were almost hypnotizing as they danced across the room. The bedroom, same as in the gathering room had swags of lush pine with the tips of snow and poinsettia above the windows, fireplace and bedframe. Wreaths of assorted pine branches and poinsettia hung by red velvet ribbon from the French bathroom doors, over the mantel, above each night stand with the most impressive one over the bed, along with one in each of the three windows. Snowman of all shapes and sizes lined the picturesque window with a three-foot Boston fir that sat in the middle with only fairy lights and red glass ornaments. On the mantel sat a ceramic nativity scene enclosed in a glass dome with white candles that nestled within the swag. Stockings were hung, and a large bowl of shiny red and green glass ornaments sat upon the coffee table. Christmas pillows of red, white and beige in assorted styles of plaids and stripes covered the loveseat and chairs along with perfect matches that lay upon the bed. The finishing touch was the blankets of red and white plaid that draped oh so spontaneously across the loveseat and at the foot of the bed. Hanna was one rarely who could not find words, but she was absolutely blown away by the images of pure love that would forever be embedded in her mind.

Hanna was in the process of turning down their bed for the night when Sam walked in. "Oh hi," Hanna spoke. "I was just getting the room ready a bit for your guests, I hope you don't mind?"

As she stepped back from the bed. Sam just stood in the doorway and smiled. "You know, you remind me of someone?"

"Who?" Hanna exhaled while speaking.

"My mom, you have a few little things about you that have stood out since meeting you is all."

Hanna walked to the other side of the bed, fluffing the down filled pillows, unsure of what exactly to say now. "This room is so full of the spirit of Christmas," Hanna replied. "I've never seen anything quite like it, and that seems to be happening a lot lately," as she reached for the remote to the fireplace taking a seat on the elegant cream love seat filled with down feathers. She felt lighter than air as she rested for the moment. "The time it must have taken to decorate, this is like something out of a movie."

Sam smiled, "Well let's start with the floors. My mother loved hardwood, so my dad and I installed this knotty oak flooring throughout the bedroom, sitting area and bathroom. The walls are a faint yellow, for it was my mother's favorite color, the bed, which by the way, is a primitive camelback four post, made of deep pine just like the rest of the furnishings in the room." His hand glided gently over the arch of the footrest. "But mom always said the bed was never complete until when you lay upon it, you felt like you were up in the clouds. Her area rugs under the bed and in the sitting area oh and in the bathroom, reminded her of when she was a little girl she once told me, so dad and I bought three, the two in here are the same and the one in the bathroom is of a much smaller scale. Yellows and rose-colored floral, same as the bed except she elected for more reds and roses with faint yellows in the background." His hand once again, running across the bedspread. Hanna just sat listening to Sam speak of every aspect of the room from the bay windows, to the white corner fireplace insert, the antique lamps, to the double pine doors that opened to the bathroom and the small quaint back porch that was just for his parents. He missed them so.

"What happened... if you don't mind me asking." Sam sat down next to Hanna, "Cancer, both within a couple of years apart, I worked at the hospital in town for 16 years, you think you know enough to save someone but, in the end, it's not up to us who lives and dies. I didn't want to see their hard work be sold out to someone who would change things here, so I went part-time and carry on the Inn for my parents." Hanna had a ton of questions that she wanted to ask but she didn't want Sam any gloomier than he already was.

Mr. and Mrs. Whittle had been left in the kitchen with Pete. "Sam, I think it's an amazing thing what you have done here and there's no doubt that your parents are very proud of you. Come, your guests are likely looking for us."

Hanna turning to Sam, "don't worry I'm not cutting you off by any means, we will finish this conversation. I'm just noticing the flame in your eyes becoming extinguished, I want you happy tonight." She placed her hand on his, held it tight, laid the remote down with her other hand and stood from the loveseat. "Come on, let me make dinner tonight for everyone." Hanna kissed Sam's cheek steering him down the hall, never letting go of his hand.

Strolling back to the kitchen Hanna smelled what seemed to be spaghetti. As they turned the corner into the kitchen she saw Pete at the stove and Mr. and Mrs. Whittle in conversation at the kitchen table. "Pete, I didn't know you could cook?" Hanna said in a humorous voice.

Pete turned slightly to see Hanna standing beside him. "Why yes," kicking his hip out, "how else do you think I've kept this marvelous figure," laughing the whole time while looking directly down at the pot of sauce.

"Oh lord Pete," rummaging through the cabinets looking for the dinnerware. "Mrs. Whittle, Mr. Whittle," Mr. Whittle looking over to Hanna. "What would you like to drink with dinner tonight?"

Mr. Whittle answered with his coffee cup in the air, "We've got our coffee and cream my dear, nothing more needed here." Hanna set the table for the five of them. She began mixing the greens of spinach and romaine for the salad, slicing tomatoes, cucumbers, and black olives. Topping it off with grated fresh parmesan cheese and Italian croutons. Sam had opened the bottle of sweet white that he had purchased earlier and began pouring a glass for Pete, Hanna and himself. Pete had placed the sauce in one bowl and pasta in another, grasping both with one hand each, he turned towards everyone, "dinner is served". They sat there for what seemed to be an eternity delighted with conversation of the olden days. Laughs were exchanged, friendships were built, love just happened naturally. Hanna had inherited a family that was not made from blood.

Dinner had been a well-deserved treat for all of them. Sam and Hanna started cleaning up the kitchen while sipping on a glass of wine. Mr. and Mrs. Whittle had made their way down the hall to turn in for the night while Pete excused himself taking a glass of wine into the gathering room where he sat in front of the fire, content with the day's memories. Halfway through cleaning the kitchen, the lights began to flicker. Sam suggested that he should get the generator going for the kitchen and asked Hanna if she would go check on the Whittles. As Hanna turned she could see that Pete had dozed off. She walked into the gathering room adding a few logs to the fire, took the throw from the sofa laying it upon him gently kissing his forehead, "Thank you, Pete, for the greatest gift of my life," she spoke with a whisper. Sam had stopped what he was doing to ask for Hanna's assistance when he witnessed the sweet gesture.

Hanna went to turn from Pete when Sam disappeared quickly from sight. Walking down the dark hallway Hanna quietly tapped on the bedroom door. "Yes, what is it?" She heard Mr. Whittle's voice in a low-key tone. Opening the door excusing herself, Hanna let them know that power would most likely be gone soon as she walked over reaching for the remote for the fireplace. "I don't want you catching a cold tonight, I thought the warm glow from the fireplace would give you enough light to see, in case you needed to get up for anything and will keep you nice and toasty during your slumber."

She turned to see the smile on Mrs. Whittle's face, "Yes, darling, thank you for thinking of us."

Hanna smiled, leaving the remote on Mr. Whittle's bedside table before exiting the room, Hanna whispered, "Good night," closing the door behind her. Hanna had just sat down at the kitchen table when the power was disrupted by the brutal storm. Besides the radiance from the fireplace, it had gone completely dark.

"Here Hanna, let me share a trick with you." He walked slowly down the hallway where Mr. and Mrs. Whittle were and pushed a button on a lamp that hung on the wall. A beautiful flame appeared. "What the...?" Hanna was shocked, forgetting this home dated back to the 1800's.

"Gas lanterns," Sam spoke out loud, "The house is full of them, did you notice the lantern on the bottom and top of the staircase? We will have light even without the electricity and all of the fireplaces in the home are gas as well except the one in the main gathering room". He took Hanna's hand guiding her to where Pete had fallen asleep. "We will leave him here for the evening, there's enough wood on the fire to keep things going at least until morning. He seems to be peacefully sleeping, if he wakes, I'll have the lanterns lit and the fireplace going in his room."

Tiptoeing through the grand entryway with Hanna by his side, he lit the first lantern in the entry, next, the lantern that sat atop the staircase banister. Making their way up the stairs and down the hall he lit one by one. Hanna never realized there were lanterns outside of every door. Upon walking into the lilac room, there in front of her were two lanterns on both sides of the fireplace with an old barn picture with lilacs in the field. Sam had one lantern left to light in the bathroom by the window. The little things she had not noticed before were just more pieces to a beautiful puzzle. Hanna, although enjoying herself, was exhausted where it had her anxiety and headache kicking in a bit. Sam watched as she took her prescription bottle from her pocket, opening it quietly not to draw attention and placing the tiny pill under her tongue.

"You ok Hanna?" Sam said with a disturbed look on his face.

"I think I'm just exhausted, but now with it being night time and no one else up here on the floor with me I have to admit, I'm a little scared." Hanna looking away from Sam and focusing on the radiance of the fireplace.

"Well, you don't have to be alone tonight if you don't want to be." Hanna looked at Sam with a jumbled look on her face.

"Sam, I barely know you."

"No, not in that way Hanna, I could stay here in the room with you. I have a couple of cots in the closet down the hall, I could just grab one of those and place it here in the room."

Hanna smiled, "You would do that, stay with me?"

"Yes, of course," Sam smiled over to Hanna. "We can have an old-fashioned sleepover, with the difference of a boy and girl instead of a girly thing, and no you're not painting my toenails." Hanna let out a lengthy laugh, one Sam had not heard during Hanna's stay at his Inn. "Well I tell ya what, why don't you get yourself comfortable. Take your clothes in the bathroom with you, run a long warm bath and get comfy. I'll go get the roll-away and my sleeping gear. I might even run down to the kitchen to make a thermos of hot chocolate. I'll grab mugs, marshmallows the works. We can just lay around and talk until you fall asleep."

Hanna glanced at Sam with such a questionable stare on her face. "Who are you Sam, where did you come from?"

Sam moved towards the door, hand upon the knob, rotating it slowly. He turned to look Hanna directly in her gorgeous green eyes, "I've been here the whole-time ladybug, I'm nothing special, just me." He exited quietly leaving Hanna to settle in for the night with questions that filled her soul.

Hanna hurried with her bath, placing her hair upon her head to not to get it wet. The tub was large, relaxing, just what she needed this night, something to help with her anxiety. She was truly a mess on the inside and the foot of snow that had started to fall was no help. Being closed in was not one her strong points, but neither was being in a town where she knew only a couple of people. Hanna finished her bath and quickly dried herself off before putting on her pink and white striped pajamas. She borrowed the slippers and the robe from the Inn before walking out into her room.

"Sam?" Hanna looked around, no Sam, however, his bed was set up closest to the door, his duffle bag tucked neatly underneath with pillows and blankets on top. She walked over to the fireplace rubbing her hands together, allowing the warmth to sink in. Hanna continued over to the winged back chair on the right this time, pulling the sage covered blanket from the back of the chair as she wrapped herself in it, legs tucked under her, head laid back to the side staring out the window. Hanna was in a trance watching the snow fall so eloquently as if each snowflake were dancing its own ballet upon falling to earth's beauty. No Christmas lights lit up the trees, no twinkle lights in the window, but it wasn't needed tonight. Time just seemed to stand still for the moment, no noise, just silent beauty.

Sam knocked at the door, "Hanna are you decent?"

"Yes, come in." Sam opened the door with one hand and holding a tray in the other.

"Are you feeling better?' Sam asked as he walked over to the bay window placing the tray upon the table as he sat in the chair beside Hanna.

"Yes, very much. Have you seen it out there? It's just breathtaking."

Hanna spoke to Sam as her head leaned back onto the chair once again, focusing back upon the falling snow. "Look at it, it's like someone is standing outside of the window sprinkling fairy dust and glitter." Sam looked out the window, pouring hot chocolate in the mugs he brought up, placing them on saucers with a couple of chocolate chip cookies and a marshmallow on the side. "It's a pretty perfect night I would have to say." Eyes fixated on the radiant flames from the fireplace that illuminated a glow upon Hanna's face.

"Sam, you were speaking earlier of your mom and dad, how you work part time still at the hospital, how are you doing it all?" Hanna spoke as she sipped on her hot chocolate, eyes heavy, just wanting to lay back against the feather downed pillows.

"Well, I wasn't going to say anything, but I'm an RN over at the hospital. I mostly deal with pediatric patients but occasionally I'm brought in on serious head traumas. I kept my job part-time so that I could keep my benefits and took on the Inn to keep it open. It gets hard sometimes. I can't seem to find help that will stay around after mom and dad passed. Mom used to do all the cleaning and dad was a wiz in the kitchen along with fixing the odds and ends around here. The two helpers we had moved on to different towns over the past year leaving me in a real bind. The other two that are on vacation right now, they work, but it's just a job to them. They don't have the heart that this place has. I love being at the hospital, it's my passion, but I also love this place." Sam looked around the room with such devotion. Hanna yawned, covering her mouth with the palm of her hand. She slowly stumbled over to the bed, eyes heavier than before. Stripping the blankets back just enough to climb into the clouds.

"I would love to help you decorate all of the rooms that haven't been touched, I have a great eye for décor if you would like the help." Sam made his way over to his cot, noticing Hanna fighting her anxiety by the quiver in her voice. He went over to the other side of the bed with his blanket and laid beside her. "Here," he said, "slide over and don't worry I'm on top of the covers." She looked up at him turning to her left side where she found herself wrapped in his arms, her head upon his chest. He was still, soaking up the time, running his fingers through her hair until she fell off to sleep.

4
SNOWFLAKES FROM HEAVEN

The wind was whipping and howling when Hanna awoke around 3 am. She had been startled by a dream that was not so kind. Stumbling out of bed quietly not to wake Sam, she sauntered to sit at the bay window for a moment wrapping the blanket back around her that lay on the chair. The snowfall had become a vicious whiteout. Her anxiety quickly trying to take over, she refocused herself. The flickering from the fireplace and gas lanterns became nurturing to her, the warmth of it feed her soul. However, her head turned back towards the window. The larger flakes were now mixed in with the smaller ones. "Snowflakes from heaven," she whispered to herself laying her hand upon the cold glass of the window. "How could I have forgotten?" She recalled what her mother use to say about rain, "Hanna, never forget that when it's raining, that's God's way of watering all of the flowers and trees to keep them beautiful like you." She remembered lying in bed listening to the tempo of the droplets against the tin roof. God's creation of her own personal lullaby.

Hanna was also recalling what her mom spoke of about the falling snow, "When winter arrives cold and blue, God doesn't forget about spring coming soon. Every once in a while, he will send snowflakes down to kiss and heal the earth's ground, washing over the land abound." She sat there recalling all the different snowfalls she had observed since a little girl. A smile came upon her face, it was some of the most memorable moments of her life. For a second, she forgot all about the snow being claustrophobic to her, the feelings of dread, no way out and focused on the memories from her childhood past. Hanna instead of absorbing any negative thoughts turned to the heavens as she glanced one last time at God's glorious gift. She was able to hold her composure, not allowing herself to go into a full-blown panic attack, instead, she recalled past joys that had been tucked deep away in the back of her mind. There was nothing to fear, she had Sam and Pete and a hospital just down the road. Hanna went back to lay in bed, snuggling deep into the covers and against Sam. She glanced over at her prescription sitting on the side table and smiled. "I won't be needing you tonight."

Morning arose, the brightness of the snow was intoxicating. Hanna left Sam lying in bed while she scurried to the bathroom to begin her new day. Sam had awoken just a couple minutes behind Hanna to the familiar sound of Christmas songs harping from the bathroom. He laid there, pillow over his head, holding on with both hands as he let out an enormous laugh. "Hanna are we having a good morning?"

Hearing Sam's voice outside the door she swung it open, towel on her head, no makeup and the plush bathrobe wrapped oh so tightly around her. "Well yes, yes we are! Did you see it out there, it's beautiful?" As she spun around in a circle.

"Someone has taken their happy pills this morning I presume?" chuckling playfully.

"Nope, still sitting on the bedside table," as she leaned over to pull clothes from her luggage bag, making her way back into the bathroom. "So, Sam, what would you like for breakfast, French toast, eggs, bacon?" Sam didn't know what exactly had gotten into Hanna this morning, but he did know he it was a relief to what he had anticipated. She was vibrant, alive, singing to her own tune. Sam laughed as if it were the first time experiencing such joy.

Hanna moved slowly over to Sam with a kiss on the cheek as he sat quietly on the corner of the bed. "Thank you for staying with me last night." She turned towards the door, opened it and began to walk into the hallway, quickly poking her head back in towards Sam, "I'll see you in the kitchen?" with that beautiful smile across her face as she tiptoed down the staircase not to wake Pete. Brushing her shoulders from the chill in the air Hanna took a detour to the gathering room where she saw Pete's humble face still off in dreamland. With a whisper and a kiss to the forehead, she managed to place a few logs upon the dying fire. "You must have fallen asleep down here last night, poor guy." She pulled the blanket up on him lightly.

Through the doorway and into the kitchen she started pulling out everything she would need to make breakfast. Hanna was preoccupied with the thoughts in her head. "Bacon, six eggs, milk, a loaf of bread, cinnamon, vanilla, where is the vanilla?" She spoke to herself. "Coffee, they need coffee," she poured hot water into the coffee pot, scooping out the tablespoons of grounds as she turned on the stove for the kettle of hot water for tea. Hanna was full of energy this morning. While whipping the egg mixture, she poured a glass of orange juice for herself, going over the details in her mind of what needed to be done around the Inn. Sam greatly needed help getting the rest of the house ready for the holidays and that's what she intended to do.

Mr. and Mrs. Whittle came strolling down the hallway into the kitchen. "Good morning dear," Mrs. Whittle commented to Hanna.

"Good morning Mrs. Whittle, how did you all sleep?"

"Like a dream," remarked Mr. Whittle as he made his way over to the kettle to pour a cup of hot water for him and the misses.

Pete must have smelled the aroma from the coffee as he was next to enter the kitchen, looking over to see breakfast in the making.

"Hope everyone slept well last night, it got pretty cold outside, but the house seems to be ok in temperature now," Sam stated as he made his way over to the coffee pot in line behind Pete.

"Woke with a chill around 4 this morning but I was so tired I forgot where I was." Pete let out a snicker.

"I covered you up when I came down this morning and placed a few logs into the fire, didn't want you to catch a cold," Hanna spoke as she was flipping the French toast. "Can't believe it's still snowing, have you heard any updates on the weather Pete?"

Sam spoke up hoping to hear they would be stuck at the Inn for a few more days. "Nope, we are just jammed, nothing is moving in or out of the area and by the looks of things, it could be a few more days.

I hope we are not going to inconvenience you, Sam?" Pete looked up from the kitchen table with a slightly apprehensive look on his face.

"Heck no, I'm enjoying having all the company here with me. It gets too quiet around here sometimes and I love having help in the kitchen." Sam placing the dishes upon the table. The Whittles, Pete, Sam and Hanna all sat down and enjoyed a hot breakfast. They found themselves laughing over the stories Pete told of passengers on the train. Mr. Whittle and Pete exchanged a war story or two and poor Mrs. Whittle, just sat there all smiles, not knowing if she was making out the whole conversation or not.

Sam and Hanna were keeping up on the kitchen, washing a few dishes here and there along with wiping down the counters. These two just seem to click, as if lost souls reunited. "So, Sam, where are the Christmas decorations kept, I'd love to get started on helping out today."

Sam took Hanna by the hand walking halfway down the hall towards his parent's room. "Well they used to be out back in the old carriage house, but my parents needed things closer as they got older. This, my dear, used to be my room, which in turn became the storage room when I moved out.

"Wow, this room must be as large as your parent's," Hanna stated looking around in disbelief.

"Yep, sure is, the only exception is there is no back porch," Sam stating moving boxes to make a path for Hanna.

"Sam, how many people do you need here to run this place efficiently and still be able to work over at the hospital?" Hanna curious about the situation.

"Well let's see, I work two 12-hour night shifts at the hospital back to back. I manage to check on the

Inn and its guests before I go to sleep on those days and before I go to work. I would really like to have two days off a week, period, with nothing to do and dedicate three days here at the Inn. Pete had strolled down to Sam's old room to see what those two were up to. He overheard the conversation that was taking place and spoke up.

"So how much would you pay an old geezer to help run the Inn for you a couple of days a week?"

"You Pete?" Sam chuckling in surprise.

"Yeah, I don't have a misses anymore, sold my old home and rent a small one bedroom just a few hours from here. The train became my wife, but it's been over twenty years and honestly, I'd like to just be in one place for the rest of my life." Hanna turned around looking at Pete with just as shocked of a look on her face as Sam had on his.

"Wow Sam, that would be amazing, but it's a lot of work, I would need to have at least two full-time housekeepers, one part-time cook, one part-time yard man and someone to oversee that everything is getting done around here on top of making reservations. Money isn't the problem, the Inn makes more than enough to have the staff back that we used to, especially if we cleaned up the old carriage house."

"Well," Hanna said, "if Pete were to run the place three or four days a week, I could run the place two days per week and help with the housekeeping services the rest of the time."

Pete spoke up, "That would cut you down to only needing to hire one full-time housekeeper, one part-time housekeeper and one part-time cook."

"Well don't forget about me," Sam said, laughing as he spoke. I would like to continue to cook on the weekends and that would give me a day during the week to keep up on the yard and landscape. Guys, I really do appreciate everything you both are talking about, but this is a different type of lifestyle, you can't just go home after a long day at the office, you pretty much live in your office, all the time." Sam not knowing when exactly to shut up.

"Let's just get the place ready for the holidays right now, we have time to discuss this later." Pete said swiftly as he helped bring out a couple of boxes from the room.

They had spent most of the day decorating two of the guest rooms, the Rose and The Lilac, this only left the Magnolia and The Lilac where Hanna was staying. Pete had taken a loft room, not designed for overnight guests with all the fancy décor, but as he said it suited him well and had an elevator that the housekeepers used. Hanna had decided that The Rose room needed a tall tree decorated in white lights with glass and opal white ornaments. The room was made up of a white couch and wing backed chair, a black wrought iron bed with pine accents, a white fireplace mantel with gorgeous knotty pine floors. The walls held rose wallpaper with a black background. "Sam," Hanna turned to him with a questionable face. "Do you mind if we keep this room simple?"

"What do you mean by simple?" Sam responded as he was rummaging through the boxes.

"Well, I don't want the decorations to compete with the wallpaper, I think keeping it simple by adding a beautiful pine swag on the fireplace mantel with white candles along with a bucket full of wood next to the fireplace will be enough to capture the spirit, a crisp white throw over the couch and at the bottom of the bed as well, also the windows, I think simple pine wreaths will be enough to hang along with some candlelight sitting on the window seals. It will add a little oomph to the atmosphere." Sam and Pete stood back taking in all the ideas Hanna was throwing at them.

"Great, I like it, simple yet it will make a statement". They had many designer pieces that they added to the already flawless room. A white and black Christmas pillow sat on the wicker chair in the bathroom along with simple wreaths in the windows and pine swags over the mirrors. Hanna worked on all the decorating leaving the tree to Sam and Pete. When it was all finished, it looked like a bedroom out of a fairytale. Hanna was so inspired, the more doors she opened, the more she was taken back.

On next, they went to the "Lilac Room". So beautiful, but just not enough room to add a full Christmas tree. "Sam, what do you think about placing a couple of small Christmas trees in metal buckets on the mantel, one on each end and a pine swag that drapes down on both sides? We can hang a beautiful oval mirror above the fireplace in between the trees with a much smaller pine swag draped over top." Wreaths of different scale were hung in the bay window, 2 larger on the outside windows and 2 smaller scale on the center windows. "We can also take down the white fabric that flows over the bed and replace that with a dark pine swag with twinkle lights, add a few Christmas pillows, a sage lap blanket over one of the winged back chairs and it will be simple, yet sophisticated and complete." Hanna full of so much inspiration, even she was starting to wear down some, but the beauty was captivating.

"Love it," Pete looking at the second smaller bedroom and bath. 'Hey Sam, do you use this smaller bedroom much?" "Um yeah, I rent it out as a double bedroom suite, there isn't much in there, I guess I need to work on that."

Hannah peeked into the open room with a four-post bed. "OK, no fireplace, but if this is used for couples with kids, I see a Santa wonderland that could take place in here with the works. A beautiful seven-foot pine in the corner, a swag of pine with sugarplums dancing over the bed, wreaths in the windows and larger one hanging from the door, one on both sides. We can even decorate the tree with lavender, lilac and green glass ornaments, keeping the theme of the main room, with a few touchups to the hall bathroom."

Sam and Pete looked at each other, looked at Hanna and back at each other again. Snickering, "I think you have a real designer on your hands here Sam", digging through the boxes, going with each idea that Hanna had for the room. The day had seemed to fly by, they decided to stop and head back down to gathering room for a well-deserved glass of wine and coffee for Pete before deciding what would be on the menu for dinner.

Mr. and Mrs. Whittle had kept busy all day helping in the main rooms. They had taken on the job of cleaning the gathering room, formal entry and dining room. They hated not being in their own home but were so grateful for Sam. The snow had just seemed to come and go all day, adding to the never-ending inches still accumulating.

Mrs. Whittle had guided her attention to Hanna, noticing that throughout the day she seemed to have picked up a cough. But as the evening progressed it became constant. "Sam if you all don't mind," looking over to the Whittles and Pete, stopping to clear her throat. "How does Chicken Parmesan sound for dinner tonight over linguine? The chicken is already defrosted and will only take about an hour." Hanna sipping on her sweet white, eyes watering, silently holding back her cough.

Mr. and Mrs. Whittle never turned down a pasta dish and Pete jumped at the chance to make a chocolate soufflé for dessert. "Well, how about I help, I'll tackle the dessert." Mr. and Mrs. Whittle were served coffee in the gathering room by Sam, as they relaxed in front of the fireplace engulfed in conversation of how Hanna was looking sickly.

Dinner prep had taken all of twenty minutes before Hanna placed her dish in the oven. With a forty-five-minute wait before topping it off with her marinara sauce and cheese, she sat down quietly at the kitchen table. Pete was busy getting his dessert ready for the second oven while Sam was assembling the counter with the dishes and silverware. He went to check on Mr. and Mrs. Whittle, making sure they were all right, not to interrupt, seeing that they were still drinking on their coffee. Sam walked back into the kitchen to see Hanna's head lying on the kitchen table. "Hey," tapping her on the shoulder, "you ok?"

Hanna lifted her head with a drab look on her face, "Just not feeling very well tonight, I think I'm catching a cold." Laying her head upon her hand, watching as Pete was doing a little dance while finishing the dessert. "I honestly don't know where you get your energy from." Coughing slightly with a smile on her face. Pete turned with a huge grin and went back to dancing while the soufflé baked.

Hanna went to rise from her chair, for the timer had gone off when Sam interrupted her. "Hey, you're not feeling well, sit. I'll finish everything." As Mr. and Mrs. Whittle came strolling into the kitchen. Everything was set up buffet style to avoid making a mess and to have more room at the table. Everyone seemed to be enjoying the meal accept Hanna. She was fighting just to swallow her food. Sam leaned over to feel Hanna's head with his hand, "Honey you're burning up."

Hanna looked over, "So that's why I'm feeling like death tonight?" "Pete, I'll be back in a few, Hanna come on, we need to get you upstairs and into bed."

"You're not going to hear me say no." Sam walked Hanna up the staircase where it was closer to her room with a lot less walking.

Supper was a success, dishes were sat in soaking water and leftovers placed into the refrigerator. Counters cleaned off along with the stove. Pete went ahead and set the timer on the coffee pot, for it to start brewing at exactly seven a.m. in the morning. Mr. and Mrs. Whittle walked arm in arm down the hall to their sleeping quarters while Pete took the elevator to the top floor. Everyone had decided to turn in early due to either being sore, tired or both from the long day.

Christmas in Hunter's Grove

5
IN SICKNESS

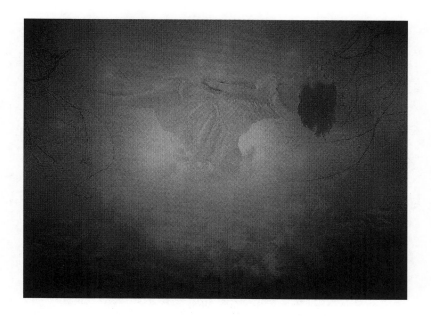

As Sam got Hanna into her room he had left her just long enough to fetch two cups of hot chocolate from the kitchen. As he entered back into the Lilac room he immediately started pulling back the comforter and sheets upon the bed. "I don't want to overstep my boundaries but didn't know if you were comfortable enough now being on your own or if you wanted me to stay with you again tonight."

Hanna, walking over to sit on the bed, shook her head. "You're asking me, because you don't want to overstep your welcome? I'm the one who feels like

a helpless child even asking for you to stay with me."
Hanna looked down onto the floor, coughing into her
closed hand.

"Hanna, I want you to know something, I think
you are an amazing woman regardless of the battles
you fight most days. You have not been a bother to
me and trust me I would let you know."

She looked up into Sam's eyes, "No you're
amazing". Coughing a little harder. She pulled her legs
up onto the bed, laying her head upon the pillow. To
achy to change into her bed clothes, Hanna just
wanted to sleep.

"Don't fall asleep, I'll be right back." Sam
scurried back down to the kitchen to gather a
thermometer and cold medicine. Running back up the
stairs, knocking before entering, "Hanna, place this
under your tongue." Sam positioned the thermometer
in her mouth and waited for the low-key beep before
removing it. "Well we have a fever, 101.4, ok I guess
we have caught something. Most likely from a
passenger on the train." He took from his pocket
medicine to help with her cough and cold placing it in
her hand. "Take these and sip on your hot chocolate."
Sam and Hanna were engaged in conversation as he
was getting the cot ready for another sleepover.
While listening to Hanna he couldn't help but feel like
a child again. The only thing missing was hand

puppets from the glow of the fire. Hanna was slowly losing interest in their chat, becoming extremely lethargic, her headache creeping back. Pulling the covers from under her, he tucked Hanna into bed layering her with a quilted down comforter.

Hour after hour Hanna's cough got worse, fever spiking higher. Sam had been up most of the evening watching over her. She had taken on quite a cold and with the weather in full force once again, it made it impossible for Sam to get situated for a good night's sleep. He had been up twice making sure that the fire did not extinguish downstairs, checking all the gas fireplaces that they were still working properly and of course watching Hanna as she slept. There was a slight popping sound as the Inn lost power. "What a time to have no electric," Sam said silently to himself. It was around three a.m. when Sam decided to climb into bed with Hanna, where he wrapped his arms tightly around her before drifting off to sleep.

Hanna awoke just long enough to feel Sam lying in bed with her. Feeling his masculine arm and hearing his slight snore, she was completely comfortable and comforted. For over the past couple of nights she had surprisingly adjusted to the sounds of the night that echoed within the walls. She took in the dulcet sound as if a lullaby was being sung just for her as she drifted off into her dreams. This night, however, would be different from the quiet slumber she was used to. Hanna was dreaming in an awake stage. She found herself unable to talk or scream. She watched as her body was wheeled out into a hallway on a gurney. Her body so heavy, as if someone or something were laying on her. Hanna found herself incapable of moving. Spirits were surrounding her, some with a sinister stare, others with whimsical smiles. Hanna was fighting in her dreams to awaken.

Without warning, she felt her body being lifted and placed in a hospital room with walls that appeared to be closing in. Hanna was somehow floating above herself. Hearing the angelic singing, familiar voices speaking amongst each other, but no words could be formed from her own lips. Sam had awoken, for he could feel Hanna moving in distress while she slept. He gently nudged her, whispering in her ear to wake up. After a few minutes, he heard a loud inhale come from Hanna. It was if life had been returned, back to her lungs. She opened her eyes sitting up, yet frozen as if afraid to move. Sam watched as her body relaxed, passing back out into the darkness of her dreams.

Hanna rolled over around ten in the morning to see Sam folding his clothes and laying them on his cot. She attempted to lift herself out of bed and instead just feel back into it. "Morning beautiful," Hanna had heard this the past couple of mornings, each time bringing a smile of comfort and love to her soul.

"Good morning Sam," coughing and now congested she asked Sam if he would mind bringing over the box of Kleenex from the sitting area. Walking across the room with the box in hand,

"Well, you certainly are not going to be doing much today, you ran a fever most of the night and must have been having some pretty bad dreams." Laying his hand on her forehead, "You're still warm, I'm going down to the kitchen to make you some tea and toast, I'll get you more medicine as well. But I need you to keep warm today and sleep as much as possible." Hanna closed her eyes as she let out a yawn. Sam kissed her on her head and exited the room. Sam spoke to Pete briefly in the kitchen while he made toast and a tea made with cinnamon and ginger.

"Our girl looked pretty sickly last night, how is she doing this morning?"

"Not any better that's for sure, she ran a fever most of the night. And I swear her nightmares scared me just watching her movements last night.

"You stayed with her last night?" Pete looked up from his coffee.

"Yeah, I actually have stayed with her for the past two nights, but don't get any ideas. The first night she was upstairs by herself and let her anxiety get the best of her, last night, well she's sick."

"No explanation needed my man, I'm glad she had you." Pete looked back down at his coffee with a smile of glee inside. "I had my computer plugged up before the storm hit, does anyone know what I might have done with it." Sam looking under the kitchen bench to see where he may have placed it.

"Oh dear, I'm sorry Sam, I unplugged it and sat it in our room out of the way of things. I meant to bring it back out but with the power out it totally slipped my mind." Mrs. Whittle spoke up as she wandered into the kitchen.

"No that's great, it has a full charge, I was going to take it upstairs to Hanna. Figured she could watch one of the DVD's from the TV room while she rested today." "So that's what's behind door number two." Pete laughing. "I just figured with the door closed it was a closet or something."

Sam sighed, "Oh lord, no, with all the weather festivities I totally forgot to give you a full tour of the home. I promise I'll get to it or you can take a tour on your own. Not going to do us much good right now, no electric and no working fireplace in that room, that's why I have the door closed." Sam chuckled as he grabbed the tray with Hanna's toast and tea. "Mrs.

Whittle, I'm going to stop by your room and grab the computer from the desk, grab a couple of movies and get Hanna situated for a while, I'll be back down in a bit.

Scanning his mother's movie collection, Sam picked out a couple of girly movies for Hanna before stopping by the Whittle's room for the computer. He took the back staircase up to the Lilac room making sure to open the door quietly in case Hanna was sleeping. "Hey, stranger," Hanna was walking from the bathroom, climbing back into bed. "Here, take this," Sam handed her two tiny pills again setting the tea and toast down on the bedside table. "I want you to drink all of this and be sure to eat your toast. I forgot I had a fully charged computer, so I brought you a couple of movies up. Thought it would help you pass the time while you rest today." Hanna looked miserable but was excited that she had something to watch for a while. "Mr. and Mrs. Whittle will be down in the kitchen most of the day. Something about baking cookies, actually, and from the sounds of it, like a ton of them." Sam laughed as he got Hanna tucked back into bed, fluffing the pillows behind her head and setting up the tray on the bed for her movie day. "I've got a lot to do today but will check on you from time to time, I'm sure Mrs. Whittle will as well, maybe even bring you up some hot chocolate chip cookies."

Hanna rolling her eyes, "Why on earth are you talking to me like an eight-year-old? I'm sick, not a kid."

"Well, that would be correct, I forget where I am sometimes, it's been a while since I've actually taken care of an adult, I'm used to eight-year-olds." Both started laughing,

"I'm sorry, I'm just miserable. Will I see you in a bit?"

"Yes beautiful, now get some rest." Sam kissed Hanna on the forehead, opened the door and gave her a wink before closing it behind him. The Lilac Room had quickly become Hanna's sanctuary and home away from home. Looking out at the beautiful snowfall made it all more inviting for Hanna to stay in bed.

Mrs. Whittle had begun her morning making more coffee for everyone and laying out all the ingredients she would need for the day. She had planned on a day of chocolate chip, peanut butter, chocolate- chocolate chip and snowball cookies to keep her busy and to keep the men's tummy's warm.

"I have a lot of work to get done if I have a chance of making an impression for Hanna to stay."

"What's that dear?" Mrs. Whittle turned with a coffee cup in her hand. "Make who stay?"

Pete entered the room. "Hanna," Mr. Whittle replied," who else do you think Sam is talking about? Someone is falling in love." Mr. Whittle sat down at the kitchen table with a grin on his face. Sam, with a shocked look on his face, as if no one in the house could see the feelings that he was trying to hide.

"No, no, she mentioned staying here at the Inn with Pete and I, but the room she is in I need to be able to rent out to guests, so I've been working on a project in my head and hopefully can use Pete's help today, maybe along with yours as well." He looked at Pete and the Whittles with his eyebrows raised, like a child awaiting an answer.

"Oh, my dear we would love nothing more than to see Hanna stay here. What did you have in mind?" Mrs. Whittle was excited to see that her non blood related family might be growing. A chance of having Hanna around to teach her old recipes, talk of old stories with and well to be able to share the closest thing to having a daughter. "Well, Hanna always talks about a cottage in her stories, not one that she has ever lived in, just how she would be so content in a small place of her own. I was thinking about cleaning out the old carriage house. Mom used it for her escape, she called it 'her little piece of paradise' it just needs to be cleaned up and things such as fresh linens, towels and oh, curtains washed. The upstairs I can get to a little day by day but with there being two bathrooms I could have the lower level complete in a couple of days". Sam got up from the table walking over to the kitchen sink to wash out his travel mug before refueling it with Mrs. Whittle's famous recipe, half hot chocolate, half coffee with a touch of caramel.

"Well, let's get to it, it's about time our little ladybug found a place to call home." Pete jumped from the table, filling his coffee mug before grabbing his coat and slipping on his boots. "Oh yeah, with Hanna under the weather, could you two check on her from time to time, I'll take a break in a bit and check on her myself as well." No words just smiling responses from the Whittles, Sam and Pete took to the outdoors.

Mrs. Whittle decided quickly she was making her garlic chicken noodle soup, enough to take care of Hanna over the next couple of days while hopefully recuperating, along with feeding the men dinner that night. She loved being in the kitchen with all the different aromas but today she was on a mission to get Hanna well and to keep the rest of them from catching whatever Hanna had picked up. Mr. Whittle under that tuff skin set up for the morning to help Mrs. Whittle out in the kitchen. The two of them together were priceless. The enjoyed each other more than second-year married couples. They were each other's favorite person.

Sam had plans to check on Hanna throughout the day, but time just seemed to get away from him. The Whittles, however, had kept her company making sure to get her nourishment up and Pete took a few rests to check on Hanna himself throughout the afternoon. From bringing her up Mrs. Whittle's concoction of spiced tea to enjoying a few moments of conversation. But mostly he found himself sitting in the wing backed chair in the bay window watching Hanna sleep. Pete had kept extremely busy helping Sam with the carriage house, watching over Hanna and making a few calls to his company. Night had fallen, Pete with still no word on the train decided to turn in early once again to get caught up on some much-needed rest. After speaking to Sam, he took his dinner and a few of his belongings to the Lilac room. Until power was back up and running he had no working source of heat in the loft and with everything going on at the Inn Pete didn't want to be the next one down for the count.

Mr. and Mrs. Whittle had taken the time out of a very busy day of cooking and washing up linens and towels to just sitting at the kitchen table by candlelight to enjoy some well-deserved time alone having dinner. Sam still had not come in for the night, the moon had risen brightly, dancing across the snow. Sam quickly looked out the window and then to his watch. He had completely lost track of time. He headed inside, leaving the warmth of the cottage behind him for another day tomorrow. Throwing his coat upon the hook and boots off at the door he saw a note sitting on the kitchen table.

Sam, Hanna has been feed and checked on most of the day. I feel she is missing her new best friend, her face lit up as the door opened, but you could just tell it wasn't us she was hoping to see. Dinner is on the stove for you, and Hanna has somehow made her way down to the gathering room in front of the fire. Oh, and Pete said he will see you bright and early. Good night my dear, XOXO

Sam was taken back as the letter was signed same as the way his mother would end her notes and letters.

Sam walked into the gathering room quietly with a tray that held two bowls of soup along with a beer for himself and a cup of tea with ginger and honey for Hanna. "Ladybug," Sam whispered quietly upon sitting beside her. "How are you feeling?"

Hanna scrunched herself up into the corner of the couch, "Feeling somewhat better, however, a quiet night's slumber without nightmares would be welcomed. I've felt so isolated today, I hope you don't mind that I brought my germs down here." She looked down at her lap, glancing up to Sam shrugging her shoulders slightly "I missed you today." The crackle in her voice rang true that she still was not better, her eyes as beautiful as ever held an emptiness as she spoke with a somber smile.

They sat in light conversation for about an hour before Sam helped Hanna up the stairs into her room. He had drawn a hot bath for her along with laying out her warmest pajamas and slipper socks, he lit the lanterns and turned to Hanna, "Go soak for a bit and I'll be right back. Sam walked softly down the hall not to wake Pete and made his way downstairs into the kitchen. Another night Hanna didn't want to spend by herself, Sam had come back up to her with no hesitation. He saw the distressed look in Hanna's eyes since he had returned from his project. Feeling almost regretful for leaving her, Sam settled in the for the evening taking care of her. Hanna was comforted in the claw foot tub, breathing in the eucalyptus that Mrs. Whittle had hung in the shower for her. Sam had made his mom's homemade hot toddy upon returning to Hanna in hopes of helping her sleep peacefully.

"Sam are you in here?" He heard her quiet voice through the bathroom door.

"Yes, I just went to get something to help you sleep tonight." Hanna came from the bathroom with a relaxed look on her face, walked over to the bed slipping gently under the blankets and comforter. "Hanna drink this, it will help you to sleep and with fingers crossed wake you to almost perfection." She reached for the cup with both hands, smelling the concoction before slowly sipping until it was gone.

"Sam, where were you all day? Not that it's any of my business, I just missed having you around." She sat the teacup on the nightstand, turned towards Sam as she nestled herself under the covers. He leaned towards her, wrapping her in his arms and stroking her hair.

"I've got a project I've been working on, I hoped to have it done today, but tomorrow it will be finished. Pete's getting up early with me, so I can be sure not to fall behind." "Anything I can help with." "Well I've got most of it covered, however, I need someone that could lay in bed and possible stitch some old curtains, maybe add your own design to them? But other than that, I've got it. I just need you to focus on getting better. I think there must be something like 6 sets of curtains, two definitely cutesy as my mother use to say and three for a man cave."

"I would love to, it would give me something to do instead of just laying here, I hate feeling helpless and more than that, feeling like I'm not pulling my weight."

"Well Ms. Hanna, Mr. and Mrs. Whittle will be upstairs in the attic with Pete tomorrow. Looks like Pete will be joining me after all in helping with the Inn." Hanna had a pleasantly surprised look on her face."

"He's staying?"

"Yeah," Sam letting out a slight laugh, I can't believe that old goofball wants to work here with me." Hanna had a pleasantly surprised look on her face as she calmly closed her eyes falling fast asleep in what looked to be pure contentment. Sam was mesmerized that even when sick, Hanna looked as beautiful as ever. He held her close in his arms as he drifted off to sleep.

Morning came, Sam had just finished getting himself ready for the day when Hanna opened her eyes. "Good morning Sam." Hanna sitting up in bed rubbing her eyes.

"Well, good morning beautiful, how are you feeling this morning?"

Hanna rubbed her throat; the soreness was gone. "Um not sure, much better than yesterday."

"Well I've got to get back to my project today, I've already gotten you your tea and medicine sitting beside you on the nightstand, Mrs. Whittle will bring you up some toast in just a bit and forget about the curtains, Mrs. Whittle knew how to work mom's old machine and had them fixed within an hour this morning." Hanna's face grew dim. "You take it easy today, do as little as possible today, meaning don't push yourself. Today's going to be a big day." Sam kissed Hanna on the top of her head, then forehead and then on her nose. "I'll see you tonight say six?" Rambling to the door. "Six it is." As Hanna buried herself back into the warmth of the blankets for a bit more slumber.

Pulling herself out of bed mid-morning, she had such excitement of working on the curtains. Now, Hanna was just eager to see what everyone was up to in the attic that was being transformed into Pete's living quarters. Hanna somehow, she had managed to forget all about Sam's project for the time being. Clothes on, hair and teeth brushed she slowly walked through the hall, down the stairs and into the kitchen. "So quiet," she calmly thought to herself. With a cup of hot tea just the way Mrs. Whittle made it with ginger and cinnamon Hanna took a banana nut muffin from the basket on the kitchen table. Life was good today, Hanna wasn't a hundred percent better, but she was much better than the day before, making sure not to overexert herself she took the back-housekeeping elevator that Sam's mom and dad had installed when they bought the Inn upstairs to the attic rooms. "Good morning," Hanna spoke softly to Mrs. Whittle who was sitting on the old brown leather sofa going through boxes of Christmas ornaments.

"Good morning my dear, you're up and moving I see." Mr. Whittle and Pete were moving old furniture into the west wing down the hall that would become the storage room. Hanna waved to Mr. Whittle as she walked through the attic almost in disbelief of how large it was.

"Mrs. Whittle, there is another whole house up here." Making her way through the doorway to the hall. Pete had designed it so that not only would he have a three-room loft apartment but there was room for storage, a room strictly for housekeeping along with two spare connected rooms with a bath in case another employee needed the space along the back side of the Inn. The three rooms that overlooked the front yard were perfect for Pete. The sunlight was warm and inviting to the space, dancing across the wood floors. The vaulted and cathedral ceiling with exposed wooden beams along with an original brick wall that ran all the way downstairs to the gathering rooms fireplace made it even more masculine than Hanna ever dreamt. He had a living area, that led into the open kitchen and dining area that shared a doorway to enter the bathroom and bedroom., both with double windows, accept the living area boasted a French door that led to a small balcony as well. A ceiling fan hung down from the masculine beams and a beautiful antique light hung over the kitchen sink. Hanna was overwhelmed by the innocence of the space. She made her way back out to the living area where Mrs. Whittle was and started folding all the fresh laundry that Pete had brought over from the wash. Hanna set up all the toiletries in the bathroom, placing a few more in the small closet behind the bathroom door. She loaded all the extras onto a cart that Pete would push into the new housekeeping quarters so that she could easily put them away. Mrs. Whittle joined Hanna as they stocked all the shelving that Pete and Mr. Whittle had put in place the day before. They shared stories, laughs and happy tears as they helped Pete build his new home. Furnishings were in place, storage was done, besides just sweeping and polishing the floors and maybe an area rug or two, Pete was home. Mr. and Mrs. Whittle called it a day around three o'clock, retiring to their room for a short nap before dinner. Hanna was busy making the bed in the housekeeping quarters and stocking the private bath.

"Hey ladybug, you've been on your feet a lot today, why don't we take the elevator down and head to the kitchen." Pete standing outside of the housekeeper's quarters waiting for Hanna.

Pete pulled out the frying pan from under the stove to make grilled cheese sandwiches while Hanna warmed up Mrs. Whittle's garlic chicken noodle soup. Hanna was feeling the effects of being up all day, Pete, however, was still going with a strong stride to his step.

"So, Pete, when are you starting here full time with Sam? Have you put in for your retirement yet and have you heard any news on when the train will be mobile again?"

"Well," Pete answered with a sip of his soup. "I wrote my retirement paperwork up last night and submitted it, in two weeks I hope to have moved my belongings from my apartment out west and be settled here with Sam at the Inn. I really thought you were thinking of staying yourself?"

Hanna looked up at Pete, swallowing a portion of her sandwich, "I really am, was, should." She was scrambling to find the right words. "There isn't much for me back west and this has been my ideal dream job for years, to help others enjoy their time."

"Well, what are you waiting for honey, it's undeniable that Sam has taken very fondly of you, it's like you've known each other for years and honestly I can't imagine life without having you around." Hanna smiled with love in her eyes.

"I've really taken to all of you as well, it's like you have been my family my whole life, but I don't wish for anyone to have to deal with me or my issues. I know I'm a real handful and I just don't think it's fair to place that upon you, Sam or anyone else."

Pete got up from the table taking his and Hanna's dishes to the sink, "Well, burden you are not and would never be, you have us and your parents not so far away from here." Pete walked back over to Hanna kissing her on top of her head, "You will find a reason to stay by the end of the day, I'm sure of it." Pete excused himself to go up to his new quarters and Hanna made her way up to her room for a short nap. Confused by what Pete had said earlier, she could only wonder what he was talking about as she quickly drifted off.

Pete listened to hear Hanna enter her room, once he heard the door close he made his way downstairs on the back stairwell, not to cause attention to himself by the elevator. He threw on his coat and boots and headed out the kitchen door to go check on Sam. "Hey little fella, you doing ok over here?" Pete shouted upon entering the carriage house.

"That you Pete?" Sam shouted down the stairs from the upper level bedroom.

"Yeah, your girl seems to be coming around some today, can't say she will be better tomorrow. I think she worked just as hard as we all did today on the loft."

Sam walking down the stairs, "Damn it, I told her to take it easy today, I don't want to freak her out but by the looks of the roads, we can't very well get out of here right now and I sure don't want her getting any worse."

Pete started laughing, "Don't you know by now, isn't no one that can tell a woman to take it easy and her listen unless she's on death's door itself?"

"Yeah, yeah, unlike me who would probably be balled up in bed till day four if given the chance." Laughing as he finished fixing the lighting fixture that hung midway down the stairs. "So, what do you think Pete, do you think Hanna will like it?" Pete took a minute to walk around the lower level. Sam had not left one thing untouched that didn't scream Hanna all over it. He left all his mom's furnishings, only rearranging things a bit to make it more comfortable.

"What do you call this, isn't this that shabby chick stuff women are always talking about?" Sam strongly laughing, "No Pete, it's shabby chic, and no I'm not girly, just lived with my mom too long." Both laughing.

"I think you've given Hanna a reason to stay."

"What to be around our dumbasses?"

"No dipshit, you have given her a home here with you, us, something she has been in search of for a very long time."

"Well, I don't want this being the reason for her staying either. But I still want to finish the bedrooms before I unveil this beauty. Hey, do you think she would like the front bedroom with the window seat or the open part of the loft? The second bedroom is too small for a master and only has a small window."

Sam looking at Pete with a confused look on his face, "Thought you said you didn't want this being the reason she stays? Oh, hell boy, the front bedroom. Make the loft into an open study or office for right now, you know how she loves to read."

Sam picked up his mom's old rocking chair, sitting it perfectly near the fireplace, placing a white throw over the top corner of the chair. "I'm just saying, I want her to stay here for me, not for what I can offer her, but for me." Pete helped Sam carry up the queen bed that had been situated in the living area placing it against the wall. "What do you say we stop for the night, see what everyone would like to do for dinner and check on our ladybug?" Yeah, I'm well spent for the day. A hot meal would do the trick about right now," as Sam trotted down the stairs.

Pete and Sam made their way back into the Inn, like clockwork taking off their shoes and coats to get rid of the frigid temps that had attached to them on such a short walk. "Mrs. Whittle, please tell me you're not cooking again, you're supposed to be my guests, not the other way around."

"The way I see it, you gave us food, warmth and a roof over our heads during this mess that has piled up outside, the Mr. and I would be in deep pooh about now had it not been for you. Plus, we never get to stay at fancy places, this has been like a vacation to us so hush up and enjoy."

"She told you," Pete, said pouring a cup of coffee. Mrs. Whittle would never say it out loud, but she missed never having children of her own, Sam and Hanna were the closest thing and she was taking advantage of it.

"Well, whatever your cooking smells amazing, or we're just starving," Sam nudging Pete in the ribs with his elbow.

"Well, go get cleaned up, I found a few extra candles, it's about time we all ate in that beautiful dining room of yours tonight.

Mrs. Whittle was eager to get back to the stove. All the boys had managed to see if anything was the mashed potatoes and what appeared to be a gravy of some sort. Mr. Whittle had made dessert earlier where it was chilling nicely in the refrigerator. Mrs. Whittle had kicked him out of the kitchen while she cooked, he had decided for once to pour himself a cognac and sip it slowly by the fire as he looked through one of the books Hanna had left on the side table. "Has anyone seen Hanna?" Sam spoke out to everyone.

Pete was walking down the hall towards the elevator, "She went to her room about 3:30, that's when I snuck back out to meet you."

Sam stopped by his old room to gather some clothes before heading up to Hanna's room. He knocked gently with no answer, softly turned the knob not to wake her. She was out cold, never heard a peep as he entered the room. Sam managed to take a shower and clean up before dinner. He wanted Hanna to sleep until the last possible moment before he had to wake her. Sam dressed in more of a casual look tonight. Brown boots, jeans freshly ironed, gray henley with a smoky blue long-sleeved shirt layered over top. Sam was finally able to clean up since the storm where his beard was looking a tad unkempt. He had gone back to his short-boxed beard style, his hair properly trimmed on the side, the way Hanna had first met him. He was fresh-faced and ready for the evening. Hanna heard the bathroom door open and the sound of footsteps walking across the floor. "Good evening beautiful." No matter what she looked like in the morning or at night, Sam always managed to call her beautiful, melting her heart each time.

"Evening? Oh my goodness its dark outside, what time is it? Sam sitting in the winged back chair, leg crossed, looked outside and back over to her, it's about six.

"Oh lord, six, you said you would be back around this time." She was messing with her hair, rubbing her face and neck with her hand, I swear I didn't mean to sleep this late, I, I......."

"What are you worried for, we just said we would see each other around six is all, why don't you freshen up and meet me downstairs? Mrs. Whittle has prepared a secret dinner for all of us tonight." Walking slowly to the door, "Oh yeah, she said we will be eating in the dining room." Smiling slightly, winking as he exited the room. Hanna was suddenly stricken with anxiety, but not the kind she needed her meds for, this overwhelming feeling was different. Sam's cologne lingered in the room, the sweet smell of vanilla mixed with leather and an earthy tone. Hanna suddenly felt like a crazed school girl, butterflies flying around in her stomach, heart pounding, fidgety, face flushed. She ran to the bathroom immediately silently giggling. She grabbed a quick shower, managing to apply her makeup and dry her hair the best she could before placing it up in a bun. Spritzed herself with her favorite magnolia perfume and chose carefully her black plaid leggings, short black boots, long black gold buckled sweater with a V-shape neckline. She carefully placed her heart-shaped earrings upon her lobes and her red Swarovski crystal heart necklace around her neck. Applying her lip gloss in the bathroom mirror, she kissed her lips together, blew a kiss and exiting her room where she walked slowly down the hall and down the grand staircase.

Peeking into the gathering room, Mr. Whittle was seated on the couch with a glass in his hand. "Well hello Hanna," she walked closer trying not to make too much noise on the hardwoods,

"Good evening Mr. Whittle, did you nap well?" Mr. Whittle nodded his head as he arose from the couch, heading towards the kitchen.

"Ok, that was weird," Hanna said out loud in a small voice. "He's been into the cognac tonight,"

Pete smiling from ear to ear laughing softly as he laid his hand upon Hanna's shoulder. "My dear you are stunning tonight, special occasion?

Hanna put her head down looking over her outfit, "Too much? Maybe I should go and change, although I'm not sure I can make it back upstairs without falling onto the bed, the dizziness has not subsided yet."

Pete looked over to Hanna, "Well Sam asked someone not to overdo it today ladybug, let me know if it gets worse, I'll take you upstairs to your room." Pete started to walk towards the kitchen, turning back towards Hanna, "Do you feel like helping me set the dinner table tonight?" Hanna smiled and shook her head in agreement of helping. The dining room was one of the areas that the Whittle's had decorated on the lower level. The table was broken down smaller for a table of six, the gas fireplace was lit along with the lanterns on the opposite wall. A seven-foot tree stood tall in the corner decorated with beautiful Victorian-era ornaments made of silk and classic glass beadwork. Some even carried the look of miniature chandeliers. White camellia flowers were tucked into the tree for extra décor along with the same that was entwined into the swag that dressed the fireplace and above the mirrors that hung on the walls. The antique serving table that upon entering the room held two Victorian style lamps with a three-foot tree that sat nestled into an antique white tin can. The four large windows that captured the moonlight held four wreaths that hung by white velour ribbon. The dining table was dressed as well with a white crochet table runner and placemats to match, the center held a long wooden box about six inches wide and four feet long, it brought together sprigs of green pine, white candles of all shapes and sizes, red and opal glass ornaments with a gold 19th century chandelier that hung from the ceiling above.

Hanna had just finished placing the glasses on the table, following Pete from one seat to the other as he laid out the plates and napkins. She followed up by adding the silverware while Pete lit the candles. Sam walked in with a serving platter filled with steaks and a bowl of sauce. Mrs. Whittle was close behind with her bowl of mashed potatoes and Mr. Whittle followed suit with his dessert and a bottle of red wine, everything laid upon the serving table with grace.

Sam turned around to look at the room, eyes focused directly onto Hanna. "My God, your stunning," he couldn't take his eyes off her and she with him. Mrs. Whittle stood looking at true love in blossom. Everyone sat down for dinner, taking a moment to give praise for the new friendships, new family, a warm place to stay during the snow event that was unfolding and the amazing meal that sat in front of them.

"Ok, everyone, I wanted to cook something special tonight, we've all been working so hard I thought it was only proper to eat together tonight as a family." Mrs. Whittle made her way over to the serving table where she announced the dinner menu. "Tonight, we are going to enjoy cherry tomato caper salad, filet mignon with a mushroom red wine sauce and cauliflower mashed potatoes, for dessert Mr. Whittle made his famous chocolate chunk bread pudding topped with cream fluff, so just don't sit there, come on up with your plates while it's hot."

Sam and Hanna looked at each other not knowing whether to giggle like two little school kids or mind their manners and get their butts up to the table. Either way, Mrs. Whittle was doing a fine job at taking on a mother, grandmother role with all of them. The dinner conversation was catching Sam up mostly of what had taken place up in the attic, minute by minute he was told of all the great progress and that with going through everything they had extra room alone just in the storage, enough actually to hold all the Christmas decorations throughout the Inn. Sam was impressed by all that had been done in a day's work.

"Just wait till you go up to Pete's man cave or in this situation the man penthouse," Hanna scrunching her forehead, eyes wide open as she spoke, "Know it's amazingly beautiful, well masculine.

Fit for a king." Pete spoke up, "Sam, I hope you don't mind but to make extra room for the storage I used many pieces of unused furniture to fix up the loft."

"Lord no, Pete, I want this to be your home, anything that was upstairs had been used previously in the Inn, my mom just didn't like getting rid of anything, so it was kept upstairs. I think this is all fantastic and honestly can't wait to see it." Sam's smile grew with emotion. "Mrs. Whittle, I never knew you could cook like this, it's fantastic." "

I have many talents, my dear, I just keep them to myself." "Well if the time comes that you and Mr. Whittle ever just want to retire from the store I could surely use your talent here at the Inn." The wine was passed around the table along with coffee before dessert was served. Hanna volunteered to gather all the dinner dishes and take them into the kitchen where she gathered the dessert plates and forks, Sam followed behind her with the left-over mashed potatoes, empty steak platter and the rest of the bowls from the table. She cleaned off the plates and loaded the dishwasher as Sam placed the leftovers into storage bowls before placing them into the refrigerator. Hanna was washing her hands off in the sink as Sam came up behind her. Hesitant to place his hands on her, he leaned over and kissed her on the neck. Hanna's whole being was affected by electricity and goosebumps. Afraid to turn around, she stood there like a mannequin in a window display. He took his hands and placed them on her upper arms as he gently kissed her neck again. She turned around to him slowly, his mouth meeting hers. His hands caressed her face, breathing labored yet heavy, her left hand wrapped around his back the other held close to his chest. It was deep and emotional. Hanna felt Sam's soul in the long yet sensual kiss. For a moment, they just melted into each other with true heated passion. He pulled her closer to him, as if that were even possible, hugging her like she had never been held. Pete walked into the kitchen at the instant that Sam leaned in to kiss Hanna one last time before heading back to the dining room.

Clearing his throat, "Um sorry guys for the interruption, Mr. Whittle is getting a bit cranky waiting for his dessert," laughing softly. "Um, I'm just going to take these." Pete grabbed the dessert plates and forks exiting the kitchen quickly giving Sam a quick wink as if to say, finally.

But as quick as the wink was given, Hanna exited the kitchen making her way up the back stairs, down the hall and into her room. She paced back and forth for what seemed to be an eternity. "I don't know him, I don't know anyone here, what kind of life will I have? Do I love him or am I in love with the idea of loving him?" Hanna had never been so confused, the problem was, there was nothing to be confused about. She knew what she felt down deep inside of her, she had new friends and a beautiful place situated amongst the Appalachian Plateau with the most amazing views, including Sam.

6
STAY WITH ME

Mrs. Whittle had cut the cake and had just finished placing each piece upon the dessert plates when Sam walked back in. "Things were looking pretty cozy in the kitchen," Pete walking past Sam gathering his silverware and dessert before sitting down at the table.

"I'm not sure, I thought she felt the same way I do."

"What are you waiting on boy, don't you see how she looks at you, can you not feel immediate love when she walks into a room?" Sam looked over at Mr. Whittle, got up from the table, grabbed dessert and hot tea for Hanna and excused himself from the room. Hanna was still, sitting in the window watching the snow fall. She was trying to think of a million reasons why she should not even be entertaining the idea of staying, but with every negative thought, the true thought of not seeing Sam again hurt her worse. She had convinced herself that this would be a night spent alone. The image of Sam became stronger the more she fought the feelings inside of her head. A tap at the door snapped Hanna out of her trance. She got up with her blanket wrapped around her, walked to the door gently turning the handle.

Opening the door, there he stood. "Sam, what are you doing?" She walked away from him glaring once again out the window. Sam sat down the dessert and tea upon the nightstand and walked over to Hanna. As he lifted his hands to place them around Hanna's shoulders she shrugged as if she knew what he was about to do. Hanna turned suddenly to Sam. "You don't know me, you don't know my past or how mean-spirited I can be at times. You have no idea what it is to wake up being me every day. Not knowing if it will be a day filled with joy or a day of dread and depression. I say things I don't mean, I'm opinionated, stubborn, some days no matter what things are never good enough. I hold grudges, get upset easily and am a monster to try and tame at times. I've had amazing days here with you and the others and somehow, it's going to be ruined, not by you or Pete or Mr. and Mrs. Whittle, but by me." Sam was taken back by the extent of how Hanna was trying to talk herself out of being where she belonged, there with him. "You're this easy-going man, shy but outgoing at the same time. You've lived in the country your whole life, you're used to a certain way of things. I'm city and country rolled into one and no matter where I am my city side of stilettos, boots and purses make me this stuck-up person to so many. I refuse to purchase my clothes where you purchase groceries, but I love walking in the rain barefoot with nothing more than a t-shirt and shorts on."

Hanna was saying everything she could to change Sam's mind on his feelings for her. With every breath, she was waiting for Sam to step into the conversation and tell her that she was right but what she was saying and how she was acting was pure torture to Sam. "Hanna, stay with me!" He had finally said it out loud.

She looked up into his eyes. "Do you mean it, you hardly know me?"

"Hanna, how do you feel about me?" She looked at him surprised by the question. "Do you not feel what I feel, did that kiss not take your breath the same as it did mine? I want to know every inch of you inside and out, I want to date you and romance you, I want to give you the perfect love."

Hanna's eyes filled with tears, "Um," reaching for words that seemed to have slipped her mind, "Are you sure? What if?"

The question stood still as He walked up to Hanna and kissed her on her forehead. "You don't have to hate me for wanting you to stay with me. I get it, you're scared. He walked out of her room closing the door quietly not to draw any attention from his guests downstairs. He found his way down the back staircase, through the kitchen and out the back door.

Pete threw on his coat and walked outside to see Sam sitting quietly in the carriage house staring at the flames of the fireplace. He knocked on the door and walked in. "She's going to leave; how do I get her to stay? I'll never beg anyone, I don't want that to be the reason for someone ever hating me."

"She could never hate you, argue with you sure, I told you from the beginning she's a spitfire, but hate, it's not in her no matter what words she throws out of that mouth." Pete walked over and sat down beside Sam. "Why are you sitting here? Get up, don't you have a bedroom to finish in this place?"

"For what, for Hanna to leave in the next couple of days? This was for her, everything I've been doing was for her."

Hanna laid up in her room reminiscing everything that had made her happy over the past few days. Not one moment in her thoughts didn't include Sam. The nightstand with the hot tea. She thought of how he took care of her while she was sick, lying in bed where he held her head up while she sipped her tea. The chocolate dessert, Hanna thought of how Sam had fed her in bed, she leaned up against his chest while eating slices of a grilled cheese or sipping soup in the winged back chair while he sat right beside her. The smell of his cologne melted her head into his pillow and the animal images he made in the dark against the flames of the fire. He found reasons for Hanna to smile.

It was around midnight when Pete made his way back inside of the Inn. Sam was adding a few finishing touches and planned on sleeping on the couch in the carriage house. Pete noticed the light coming from Hanna's room and could hear her talking to someone. He knocked lightly to see Hanna's face as she opened the door. "Pete, what are you...."

"No, the question is, what are you afraid of?" I'm not going into detail but what that boy has been doing over the past 48 hours is nothing less of a miracle, that miracle being for you. So, what, you used to travel, you used to have a high flatulent job, eat at expensive restaurants and stay at five-star hotels. Question is, do you now?" Your words young lady can cut like a knife, they cut the people that don't deserve it, the ones that would give you every morsel of food they had left and their last stitch of clothes if it meant you were nourished and protected. You really lit Sam up, are you that afraid to love that you have to hurt him to be able to walk away?"

Hanna broke into tears, "I'm scared, I don't want him to love me, everyone that loves me leaves me. I don't want to lose him too." Pete saw the honesty in Hanna's eyes, he understood a little better why she was trying to push Sam away. "Well, I didn't mean to upset you and surely didn't intend to make you cry. You have a great guy that fell into your world, that kind of thing just doesn't happen Hanna. God's watching over you, he's giving you exactly what you have been missing. Understand, Sam is the missing piece to your puzzle." Pete smiled at Hanna, kissed her on the forehead before clutching the doorknob, exiting the room. Hanna changed into her pajamas, took a sip of what had become cold tea and slipped into bed looking out the window to see the light from the moon glistening against the snow filled trees. Sam's pillow was tucked snuggly under her head and chin, laying it just right as if he were laying under her.

His scent that still lingered helped her to fall asleep, but the pillow wasn't Sam.

Morning had come, the snow had finally stopped. Even through the curtains, the sun mixed against the snow that streamed stunning light into the room. Hanna heard a vehicle for the first time since the beginning of the snow. She scurried to the window to find a snow plow making its way down the road. For a moment, she had forgotten all about how much of an ass she must have made of herself the night before.

A quiet knock sent Hanna rushing to the bedroom door. "Sam, oh," Her head hung low making her way back over to the sitting area to watch the snow plow drive out of sight.

"Nope, not Sam but he did send me up to see if you wanted to take a drive. We're headed to the shelter this morning, something about him and the owner speaking and needing to find homes for the animals. Mr. and Mrs. Whittle are even tagging along."

Hanna looked over to Pete, "How can anyone even want to be around me after last night?"

Hanna glanced into Pete's eyes. "You had a bad moment, we all have those, we just learn to forgive and forget, don't we?" Hanna looked at Pete with tears in her eyes. "No need for that again this morning, we have dogs to save. Now get a move on little lady, I'll meet you downstairs in the kitchen in about thirty minutes." Hanna had no time to throw any sort of a pity party, she smiled at herself in the mirror and began getting ready for her new day. A hot shower would do the trick, every ounce of bad energy seemed to wash away from her soul, she found herself singing as she dried off, using her hairbrush as a microphone like she did as a little girl. Dressed, hair dried and thrown up in a hair clip with a light application of makeup, just enough for her eyes to shine. She grabbed her wristlet, placed her medication in her pocket and down the hall she went.

Upon entering the kitchen, she overheard Pete telling Sam to take his time. "Take your time about what Sam?" Hanna peeking into the kitchen.

"Well we were all going to go but the phone lines are back up and there must be twenty calls that need to be made. Pete is going to stay here and take care of returning all of them and Mr. and Mrs. Whittle have already started cleaning the entry and the gathering room. We have guests arriving in a few days, we're back up and running."

"Well, should we stay here and help, there's a lot to do over the next couple of days."

"No, we won't be gone long, I promised Janice down at the shelter that I would pick up a list of the pups in need of a home to have here at the Inn, we actually adopt out a few a year from my, I mean our Inn," glancing over to Pete.

"Get your coat, I've already had the truck warming up for a bit now." Walking down the freshly shoveled walkway and to the truck. Hanna's dream town had quickly become a ghost town, old buildings with no life stood beneath over two feet of snow. Windows, dark and gloomy, yet beautiful in its own curious way but this heightened Hanna's anxiety. She felt as if they were the only two people left on the planet at this very moment. She reached into her jeans and pulled out her prescription. "You ok," Sam observing Hanna.

"Yeah, just feeling a little overwhelmed is all." Sam not saying another word turned his head back to the road. "How far away are we going?"

"Making the next turn onto Bennett and then we will be about a minute to go." Hanna sat quietly but happily content knowing they were just a minute or two away. Sliding into a parking spot Sam jumped out of the truck making his way over to Hanna's side and opened the door. "Let's go." Sam grabbed Hanna's hand to help her out of the truck and kept a hold of it onto the sidewalk and into the door. Janice greeted them as they came into the reception area.

"Sam, it's nice to see a human, I didn't think the snow was ever going to stop". She shook his hand and introduced herself to Hanna.

"I've got twelve pups I would love to find homes for soon, I've got pictures along with any information on each of them for you and even placed them in a binder ready to go.

"May I?". Hanna reached out for the binder looking at each pup while Sam and Janice were in conversation. "Cloe, oh my goodness, she's a doll baby." Cloe was a mixture mostly of a Maltese breed and teacup size at that. Her white fluffy fur blended in perfectly with the snowfall, she had the most beautiful little eyes and a tiny button nose. Sam and Janice looked over at Hanna where Sam captured a moment of peace in Hanna's face.

"Would you like to see her?" Janice responded waving her hand down the hallway. Hanna looked over at Janice,

"No, I would most likely fall in love and well, I'm traveling right now, and my parents would never approve of me bringing a dog into their house. Sam watched Hanna's expressions turn from pure love to a depressed state.

"Well, I would like to see her, if that's ok?" Janice took the hint easily, they made their way down the hall into an open room full of old children's furniture such as chairs, small beds and even mini sofas. The walls were painted a soft sand color with trees and flowers painted upon them with tiny paw prints as the leaves and petals. Twelve puppies greeting them as they walked into the room.

"This is so cool, I thought they would all be locked up in individual cages". Hanna stood in amazement. "You really take great care of these little ones," Hanna dropped down to her knees where her lap quickly became overflowed with these little miniature beings. She was laughing like a little child, then all the sudden in the mixture out popped Cloe's little head. "It's Cloe," Hanna scooped her up in her arms receiving a million kisses from such a tiny little soul. "Oh, my goodness, she's amazing, looking up at Sam with a huge smile and bright eyes. Sam knelt to pet her and while Hanna was embraced in the moment of puppy kisses. Sam looked up to Janice nodding his head in a way that Janice knew he would be back later to pick up Cloe.

"Well Janice it's been great seeing you, but I left Pete and the Whittles back at the Inn to help out with some much-needed work. I really need to get back to them." He helped Hanna up from the floor, picked up the binder for the Inn and grabbed Hanna's hand walking to the front door. "Oh wait," Sam poked his head back in the door. "Janice, you know, Mrs. Whittle has gotten together tons of blankets and towels that I can't use any longer for our guests, what if I bring them by to you around seven?" Janice shook her head in agreement.

Sam opened the door for Hanna, helping her back up into the truck. On the drive back to the Inn Hanna glared out the side window, not paying any attention to where she was going, or the views she was missing, she just sat in silence. They pulled back into the driveway, exiting the truck and back inside the Inn. "Hanna dear, would you help an old lady out by mopping the entryway, my back is really acting up today."

Hanna heard Mrs. Whittle's voice coming from the front of the Inn, she turned to Sam, "Thanks for getting me out for a bit," she took the shelter book from Sam's hands and headed towards the check-in area.

"Sam, perfect timing, I just finished hanging the rest of the pictures in the carriage house, I don't think there is anything left to do, it's perfect". Pete walking towards Sam,

"I hope this all works out, if not I guess I can take over the carriage house and have another room here to rent out."

"What in the world are you talking about boy, that girl loves you, she knows she does, she's just scared and full of those women's emotions," Pete's hands flying all over the place.

"Well can you keep Hanna busy for a bit, I told Janice I would be back by around seven tonight but I'm going to call her now to slip back out there to take the blankets back down to her and pick up Cloe. Regardless if Hanna stays or not, we need a four-legged little one around this place."

Pete nodded his head in agreement and kept his word by keeping Hanna busy. For the next couple of hours, Hanna worked on polishing the wood in the entryway and up the grand staircase. Mr. and Mrs. Whittle went into the kitchen to gather up a surprise picnic for Sam and Hanna while Pete kept busy on the phone returning the many calls as promised from the front desk. On Sam's way, back down to the shelter he stopped and visited Ms. Sue for a moment, she was a great florist in town and one of Sam's parent's best friends back in the day. He wanted an extra-large arrangement of fresh flowers made up of white camellias and roses. Sue told Sam that she was amazed the generator had kept all her supply of flowers stunning and still intact during the storm. They walked into the back of the shop where Sue gathered the flowers, cutting and arranging them as they stood there in conversation. "Well Sam, I hope whomever this girl is she realizes how lucky of a young lady she is." Sue handed the beautiful spray of flowers over to Sam.

"These look amazing Sue, but who said they were for a girl?" Laughing as he started walking towards the door. "I'll be back in a couple of days to help you out with shoveling your front walk. Need to get the doors open in town as soon as we can. See ya soon Sue, if you need anything give me a ring." All Sam could think about is what Hanna would say tonight as he presented her with his special gift. He pulled up in front of the shelter. Turning off his engine he gathered the blankets and towels before hopping back inside. Janice had just given Cloe a bath and was in the process of drying her when Sam stepped into the back room. "I can't believe you're finally taking one of the pups, thought you said your life was too busy for a dog?"

Sam looked over at Janice, "Well it was, but I've got Pete at the Inn now, which I need to introduce you two and if all goes well hopefully Hanna will be joining Cloe and me at the Inn."

"Well she is a delight, and she must be something pretty special to have gotten your attention. The Sam I know hasn't had the best of luck in the dating scene. But do you think it's too soon after Caroline?"

Sam shrugged his shoulders, "Well no one at the Inn knows about her, worst five years of my life that I would like to leave behind me. I didn't see this one in the cards, that's for sure."

"And you're not supposed to," Janice fastening a collar made up of pink rhinestones around Cloe's neck. "Well, here she is, pretty as a picture, oh wait" Janice reached into the drawer under the grooming table and pulled out a pink hair bow placing it gently onto Cloe's little head. "I know the stores aren't open quite yet, so I put together a week's supply of puppy food, her favorite toy and a leash to match her collar. I have some puppy sweaters up front for sale if you want one, Christmas is coming."

Sam rolled his eyes with laughter, lord what has this world come to, diamonds and sweaters for dogs? "I think I'll hold off on that one for now, with any luck Hanna can come by next week and pick her own little closet out for this little fur ball. Put this toward the bill." He handed Janice fifty dollars for the adoption fee along with another hundred so that Hanna could come back and shop for Cloe. Janice gave him and Cloe a hug goodbye as they made their way back out the door. "Well see you next week," Sam yelled as he got into his truck.

Sam took a detour back to the Inn to check on the Whittle's store, along the way he found himself talking to Cloe. "Well girl, you are the one for Hanna and hopefully Hanna will see she is the one for me." He rubbed her head and spoke softly to her the whole way back to the Inn. He pulled up but not close enough to give it away that he was back. Sam exited the truck with Cloe in his arms along with her goodie bag packed by Janice. Sneaking back into the carriage house he welcomed Cloe home. He spent the next hour getting her acquainted with her new surroundings, he had already shoveled a small spot out by the door, so she could do her business and laid a couple of puppy pads down in the kitchen near her food and water bowls. He sat fidgeting in front of the fireplace playing fetch with Cloe. She seemed to be fitting in quite well, melting Sam's heart with each tiny yap. She found her bed, which was nothing more than an old oversized cream pillow that he had laid near the fireplace. Before he knew it she was fast asleep.

He called Pete's cell and asked if Mrs. Whittle had finished her famous sausage tortellini. "It has this whole house smelling like an authentic Italian restaurant. I've already taken my dinner up to the loft and Mr. and Mrs. Whittle took theirs into their room for a cozy fireplace dinner tonight. I'll meet you at the back door." Sam trotted down the walk to meet Pete, "There's bread, salad and a bottle of Hanna's favorite white wine in the basket, all you have to do is warm up your dinner. Did you pick up pipsqueak?" Pete speaking in a whisper not to draw attention from Hanna.

"Yeah, she's amazing." "

We're talking about the dog, right?" Pete letting out a slight laugh. Now go, Hanna is in the sitting room a little tired I think, I've had her cleaning the past few hours. I'm heading up for the night, catch up tomorrow and if you need anything just call." Pete pushing Sam out the door.

Sam made his way back to the carriage house to put the food away, looking at the dining room table he decided to use the coffee table for his and Hanna's first dinner alone. Designed with red candles and his mom's white china with a seamless view of the fireplace, "A perfect spot," he thought to himself, praying for a good outcome to his question to Hanna. Cloe was still passed out, so Sam plugged in the Christmas tree, lit all the candles on the fireplace mantel along with all the lanterns on both sides of the doors and windows. He turned the gas lights on that framed the stairway to give off just enough light for

Hanna to see what he had been up to. On his walk back to the Inn, he plugged in the Christmas tree that stood decorated with colorful lights near the edge of the house. For the final touch, Sam lit candles that were placed in bags along the walk to the carriage house.

The night had gotten quiet, almost still, with no movement amongst the Inn. Sam trekked into the kitchen tiptoeing towards the gathering room. He saw the silhouette of Hanna sitting silently amongst the walls by the fire, sipping on what he guessed was a glass of her sweet white. The dancing of the flames against Hanna's skin put off a stunning amber glow. "Gorgeous," Sam spoke quietly. After last night's adventure, he thought for sure she would already be in her room for the evening.

"Busy on your project again today?" Without turning her head, she knew it was Sam standing close by. The brushing of his feet against the wood floors, no matter how silent he tried to be always gave away his entrance into a room.

"Yes, actually. I've managed to do a two-week project in two and a half days along with a couple of bonuses." Hanna with a confused look on her face was greeted by Sam's hand as he helped her up from the couch. "I was taking a chance on you still being up tonight. Thought maybe you had retired to your room with the rest of the house."

Hanna smiled at Sam, "No, I could not go to bed without seeing you. I made a complete ass out of myself last night, nervous, afraid, alone, full of stored up energy I guess from being in such a soul-consuming storm, I lost it. I am so, so sorry." She could not move her eyes away from his, hoping he would lean in and kiss her the way he did last night in the kitchen. Her body was yearning for his electrifying touch.

"I want to show you something, it's not much but it's a start. Sam reached for Hanna's hand pulling her up from the couch holding her body to his, without hesitation he let go, grabbing her hand leading her to the kitchen. "Come on, we need to get bundled up, it's freezing outside."

"Outside, as in out there." Pointing with her finger. Sam smiled helping her to put on her coat. She leaned over to place her boots on as Sam was twirling her scarf around her neck and placing her toboggan onto her head.

"OK, are you ready?"

"Sam, what have you done?" Burning with excitement Sam opened the back door to reveal a light in the darkness. Hanna's eyes grew huge, the child inside of her brought out the enchanting childlike spirit she had been lacking for years. Luminous paper lanterns lite the freshly brushed walkway to reveal perfectly laid brick. Before her stood a beautiful pine, it must have been over twenty feet tall, beaming with colorful lights. The snow and icicles glistened in the moonlight as they dangled from delicate tree branches. The walk was charming but what would soon stand in front of her was far from any dream she had ever had. She was captivated by the sheer exquisiteness as she came upon the carriage house decorated in white fairy lights. The carriage home was grand in her day, little wear but still stood soft, elegant yet strong. Sam took Hanna's hand and kissed it, "This is what I've been up to, I could not imagine a more deserving person than you to give this gift to."

"Gift?" Hanna looked at him with a shocked look in her eyes.

"I asked you yesterday, would you stay with me? I'm right here Hanna, right in front of you, I've fallen in love with you and would love nothing more than for you to be mine." Hanna looked away from Sam and focused on the carriage house for a moment. It was barn shaped with white brick and black shutters, the once wooden carriage doors in the front had been permanently closed but the architecture was kept in place. The window openings above were gorgeous, triple pained with flower boxes that hung below. Ivy swept across the sides with a chimney that peaked out from the gambrel roof. Sam swung the side door open to an indoor winter wonderland and a special present to go along with it all as a finishing touch. Hanna crossed the threshold to see a ten-foot Douglas fir decorated and trimmed in assortments of white. The floor to ceiling windows brought the outdoors in. Hanna heard a whimper, "Sam, did we let something in?" quietly peeking around.

"No, but I did." He walked over by the fireplace and picked up Cloe, she was alone when I took the blankets back to Janice earlier, she needs someone like you and you absolutely needed someone like her." He got down on his knee and instead of a proposal this is what Hanna heard. "Hanna Paige Montgomery, it's been a long time since I've had feelings for another human being, much less a little fur ball like Cloe. You are full of ups and downs and I'm pretty sure I've experienced some of your ins and outs as well, but it's what makes you, well... you. I love you, I want to learn about you, grow with you, take you on dates and snuggle by the fire. I want to get to know you, what makes you laugh and not make you cry. So, I'm asking one last time Hanna, will you stay with me?" Hanna's eyes welled with tears, swallowing what felt like a golf ball in her throat, he was truly sincere in everything he was saying. She could see it and feel it.

Hanna slipped over to Sam, knelt beside him, petting Cloe on her head. "Yes, yes, of course, I'll stay. I can't promise all great days, but I sure will try my hardest. He placed Cloe down upon her pillow and stood up bringing Hanna up with him. He embraced her with one arm locked around her waist bringing her body tightly against his. Sam's right hand upon her face, gazing into her eyes, her heart was racing, palms sweating, she leaned in further with her eyes closed to feel his breath on her neck, the sweet leathery smell of his cologne overloaded her senses. With a slightly open mouth, he kissed her neck, hard, strong and deep. He came around to her face kissing her forehead, left cheek and down to her mouth. Slow and succulent his moist tongue and soft lips took her breath away. That electrifying feeling overwhelmed her senses, something she had never quite experienced.

Captivated by his strength, his kiss was intense, but she could feel he was holding back. The kiss became sensual, soft and romantic before he pulled away, looking into Hanna's eyes. "I've got dinner for us, why don't you stay in here with Cloe and get familiar with your new home." Hanna stood there dazed for a moment before picking up Cloe. She smelled of fresh strawberries and had the most adorable face she had ever seen. Hanna held her close to her as she looked around the living room. The wooden mesquite hardwood floors contrasted against the southern chestnut windows along with the large matching wooden beams that lead to the ceiling, they were strong stretching across, the fit tight and stern. There were three lantern style gas lamps that hung from the ceiling along with one on each side of the window and one next to the door. Same as in the Inn, the lantern style lamps were at the bottom of the staircase connected to the handrail and what seemed to be one at the top. The furniture was placed precisely to not block the view of the fireplace or the floor to ceiling windows. The sofa was white with soft and bold roses splashed into the fabric. Solid cream cashmere throws laid over the couch and loveseat with pillows to match. A maple coffee table sat in the middle of the grouping where Hanna noticed the red candles and white china. There were no curtains, as the back of the home faced a forest of trees and what appeared to be a small stream. The room and its surroundings were perfect. The old fireplace was built of large stone from floor to ceiling, over twelve foot tall, it had a thick wooden mantel built into the stone that held an assortment of glass candlesticks and white candles, on both sides of the fireplace Sam had sat up wooden trays that held groupings of white candles, alongside was a large oval basket with a white crochet blanket and a sage cashmere one that hung perfectly over the side. There were no walls, just a fireplace, open on both sides that separated the kitchenette from the living room. Hanna loved the open concept, she hated her apartment because it made her feel closed in, but this home was different. Smaller in diameter but spacious in its luxuries.

The long stairway lead to the loft up above, not sure how long Sam would be she situated herself on the couch with Cloe taking in every detail that Sam had put into this special place that she was going to call home. Sam walked into the living room with dinner on a platter, he set it down carefully in the center of the table and poured both a glass of wine. Sam lit the candles and laid Cloe down on her bed with her chew toy. "Mrs. Whittle made this for all of us tonight, she sent ours over in a picnic basket, I guess you can say this is our first date even though we've already slept together all week."

Hanna blushed, "Hence the word slept. I can't believe you did all of this." "Well... we, Pete, helped me the past couple of days, he actually got the rest of the pictures hung up on the walls while I was gone getting Cloe."

"Well, now that you've got us, what are your plans?"

Sam sat there for a moment. "To never stop loving you!"

Hanna's eyes smiled with love, "No silly, your plans for the Inn? You have guests coming within the week and only Pete and I here to help for now. Plus, Pete and I need to move our things, cancel our leases, utilities and whatever else I'm forgetting now."

He saw that excited yet fearful look in Hanna's eyes. "Let me ask, do you have any friends in your building?"

"Yes, I've got two girls that live underneath me and they have a key to my place, not to mention I could give them a lot of stuff from my place, you know help them out."

"Ok, do you need any of your furniture? Besides your clothes and personal items, what else do you want? Make a list tomorrow, do you think the girls would be willing to help you out?"

Hanna took a bite of her dinner, "How far, drive time are we away from my home?" Hanna pulled out her phone and mapped it out. "Four hours, four... really? It took me forever to get here by train."

"That's a one-day trip, I've got my truck and Pete and you're only two hours away from where Pete lives, talk about convenience. Out of every state, you both live in the same one." Sam shook his head, looking up at the ceiling as if to say nice joke, God. "We could take off on Friday be back on Saturday and have four days to get the place together."

"Do you think Mr. and Mrs. Whittle would stay here while we were gone?" Hanna asked with a questionable look in her eyes.

"I'll have to ask them, but most likely yes."

"Once we are back, what do you need us to do, can you afford to pay Pete?"

"Um, Hanna, do you not remember us going over all of this? We have a perfect schedule until I can find two part-time housekeepers. We're gonna be a little busy, maybe some minor stress, but nothing that we all won't be smiling about at the end of the day." Sam was being observant to Hanna's quietness and forgetfulness. He lifted her head with his finger, looking into her gorgeous eyes. "Besides I need you focused on planning the events for weddings and parties here on the grounds. I think your gift is the perfect fit. Once we get up and running with those bookings, I'll bring on a third housekeeper and another weekend chef, so that you can put your talents to work."

"You have this all mapped out?"

"Yeah, pretty much, just following the old layout of how it was before when mom and dad ran the place, it worked really well."

"With four rooms to rent out, are you sure you can pay everyone?" "Well I thought about that also, there are two bedrooms in this home, we could share the home and I could rent out my room for guests with special needs or for a couple who just prefer to be on the lower level. I also have mom and dad's room that I could rent out as well. That would give us six rooms, they're already decorated, all they would need would be names. I stay booked seven days a week from the beginning of November through the middle of March. This snow storm being a fluke, between the holidays and skiing, I'm situated in a prime location."

"Wow, this is all so amazing, I still have to call my mom, lord she is going to be pissed."

Sam smiling, "What did you do?" Hanna looking with squinty eyes towards Sam.

"Let's just say we traded in your train ticket for two due to the encumbrance this trip caused and as a part of Pete's retirement he gets 24 round trip tickets per year to use anywhere he would like to go. Your parents are already in the books for the week of Thanksgiving and for Christmas."

"My parents are coming here?"

"Yep." With a loss of words, Hanna just sat there minding her own business for the moment and ate her dinner.

"How did you talk to my parents?" As much as she tried to stay focused on dinner, her mind was in a million places. "Listen, I took a leap of faith, and got your mom's number out of your phone one night in case of an emergency. But I called her yesterday and told her I was completely in love with you and wanted you here with me. We talked about two hours, I told her that if your answer was no she would see you in a couple of days and that I would be sure to have you on the first train out, but I asked her if you stayed that I would love them to come here, all expenses paid, of course, to spend the week with their daughter and get a chance to know me and your new surroundings."

"She said yes to all of this?" Hanna was so confused, her mother never agreed to anything immediately.

"She said yes, so Pete and I booked their tickets, we knew we could cancel them if need be."

"Sam Michael Hanson, that's right, I did a little investigating of my own. You have thought of everything, especially getting my mom to relax, I still can't believe all of this. You and Pete are definitely partners in crime." Rolling her eyes as she brought her glass up to sip on her wine.

"Yeah, and we are two peas in a pod, so what's your point?"

Hanna giggling "I don't have one."

"Exactly, so just hush." They sat for the next hour going over all the plans that they would talk to Pete about in the morning. Enjoying the bottle of wine and good conversation.

Christmas in Hunter's Grove

7
CAMELLIAS AND ROSES

Sam got up from the floor collecting the plates off the coffee table. Cloe had all but decided that she was going to take over Hanna's attention for a bit. Her tail wagging in circles, tongue lapping against Hanna's cheek. She was showing her appreciation of having a home and having a human to love. With Cloe being so young she was like a newborn baby in the household. The times that she was awake were crazy, fun and loving. She was full of energy and wanting to be showered with affection, but she seemed to have more sleep time than being alert and wakeful. Hanna placed Cloe on her leash to take her outside, getting her used to doing her business where she was supposed to.

Back in the door, they came, scrambling to the fireplace to shack off the cold. Hanna picked up her glass from the coffee table and walked into the kitchen, poured another glass of her sweet white, smiled at Sam and leaned up against the counter. "Cloe has fallen back to sleep on the couch. I still can't believe you went back and got her."

Sam turned to Hanna, dish soap on his hands as he reached for a towel. "She needed you and you needed her. I could not think of a better partner to have around the house when I am at work to help keep your mind focused on something else besides your anxiety. She will be a part of the Inn while you're at work and home with us at night."

"You know there were twelve of these little guys that needed a home, they all seemed to get along so well at the shelter, do you think Pete would want to adopt one? Hanna looked up at Sam with a warm smile.

"He has often spoken about the dog he used to have but could not keep him due to traveling with his job." Hanna watched Sam's expression.

"I don't know, if we found a little one like Cloe at least they would have a familiar playmate and the Inn hasn't been the same since losing Duke. Our guests were always used to having him around the place."

Hanna turned to walk back into the living area. "You know when I was scrolling through a few pages from the shelter book I came across a little delight that would fit Pete's personality."

"Which one?" Sam had come back into the living room sitting next to Hanna where she had cuddled up against him, knees up on the couch, laying between his arm and shoulder.

"His name is Charlie, He's a chocolate colored Cocker Spaniel. Masculine, fun loving and cute as a button. I would love to surprise him with this little fella, what do you think?"

Sam laughing "Well I guess if he doesn't like his surprise we would end up with our own little king and queen here at home, sounds like you like him as well. But I do remember him, he is a handsome little fella. I can call Janice to see if we can come to get him tomorrow."

"That would be so amazing, and not handsome, he's cute." Hanna leaned over to pick up Cloe, carefully placing her on her stomach before nestling back into Sam's arms where she pulled them around her. "I still can't believe you did all of this, Sam it's absolutely incredible that you took such a chance on me. I've never had anyone in my life to do the things you have done, I'm not even completely deserving of all of this." Sam took his hand, running his fingers through Hanna's hair.

"Well, where would you have gone, back to your apartment? Hanna, you just fit perfectly within these walls, within the Inn. Your personality and love are just what this place needed and what I needed without even knowing myself." Hanna melted deeper into Sam's embrace. They laid there with the warmth of the roaring fire, gazing past the windows to the somberness picture that was created for this exact moment.

"It's snowing again." Hanna laid in comfort as she spoke to Sam.

"Yep, but not for long, it's coming down too slow to be anything to worry about."

"It's breathtaking," Hanna was at peace, watching the snowflakes dance as they slowly descended, landing upon the already snow-covered branches of the trees. It was hypnotic and restful, she could not remember the last time she had felt or experienced such silence or peace. Sam laid against the throw pillows still stroking Hanna's hair, without saying a word, both were immersed in a private moment amongst themselves.

"I know we are comfy and all, but I never showed you the rest of your home. So, do you want to see the rest of your place?"

"You mean our place," Sam looking down to see the smile on Hanna's face. He wasn't expecting to hear the words, he could still hardly believe that she wanted to be with him. Sam sat Hanna up on the couch, took her hand raising her from the couch and lead her upstairs. "I know you love to read and honestly besides putting in a home office I wasn't quite sure what to do with this space, so I put up some cross banisters along the bottom to keep Cloe safe and made this into a quiet reading area when you get stressed or just need a little downtime. Earphones, MP3, everything you need to just unwind, oh not to mention the natural sunlight, to keep you from feeling claustrophobic and you can see the Inn from here as well." She was amazed by the detail of such a tiny space. It held a large window seat with a white flowing cover and a coffee table to match, Candles, sequin silver pillows with oversized lush purple and lavender ones. Even Cloe had her own quiet spot. Oils, lotions, eye mask, it was all there. Including Hanna's favorite flowers of white camellias and roses. The crystal chandelier that hung from the vaulted ceiling, it was the finishing touch. She imagined what it was going to feel like being tucked up in her private space.

Her whole body was overwhelmed with the feeling of love, the house gave her a calmness that was new and welcomed. A catwalk also overlooked the living area that held two doors at the opposite end. Sam opened the door at the end of the hall first, the smaller of the two bedrooms. "This one I will take for now, it's a smaller room but can at some point hopefully be put to better use." Hanna slipped Sam a smug look.

"Here is your room." He opened the door to capture the moonlight streaming into the window through the luscious billowy silver curtains, the pillows were the same as in the loft, it was if the snow were dancing a waltz in her chamber. "Magical," Hanna took in a deep breath and exhaled slowly, "Camellias and roses, how in the world did you know they were my favorite flowers?" A lush bouquet set on top of the dresser with a smaller display upon the fireplace surrounded by candlelight.

"It wasn't hard to figure out, your cell phone case is roses, white to be exact and your screen saver has a beautiful picture of white camellias." The window was a large window seat like the one in the loft with a white down filled cushion, lined with silver sequined and silk lavender throw pillows, the ones on the bed matched perfectly. The bedspread was a shimmery silver with two large shams, they also matched the curtains that flowed to the ground. The sheets were a soft lavender, almost washed out, but beautifully put together. White washed dresser and nightstands sat on maple hardwood floors with a white fluffy area rug tucked underneath. There was a gorgeous freshly painted white fireplace that sat against the wall opposite the bed, a sun inspired silver plated mirror hung over the top with large rhinestones on the tips of the sunbeams along with evergreen and candlelight upon the mantel.

Hanna felt as if she were living inside of a dream. A perfect dream with the love of her life. Every ounce of her was within this home. Her body was full of electricity and with a quiver in her voice, fighting back the tears she managed to get out a thank you to Sam. Sam took Hanna's hands and placed them around his neck. His right hand pulled her close, no space was wasted in between them. He hit a button on the nightstand that was connected to the stereo system within the house. Hanna's right arm was brought down entwined with his. Her left hand upon his shoulder, his right hand and arm not leaving its original spot, only pulling her in more profoundly. Swaying back and forth his feet stepping towards and away with Hanna's footsteps to follow. Sam started singing along to the soft jazz that he had downloaded to a personal playlist just for Hanna. He spun her slowly to land in his arms, twirling her back out to only pull her back ever so gently. She could feel every muscle underneath his clothes. They stood there in silence. Sam was trying to fight with everything he had, reaching deep within his being not to kiss her. He wanted more, but this was not the time.

Hanna was overwhelmed. She was so lost within Sam that she felt overpowered by his existence. The magnetic tension between them could be felt in her soul. He wanted her right there, he imagined ripping off her clothes and dropping her to the bed, but that wasn't his style. Hanna was imagining his sultry kiss and became weak in the knees at that very moment. Her heart was racing, breathing labored to his every touch. He leaned in towards her, touching her bottom lip with his tongue and tugged on it ever so gently as she opened her mouth wanting more. His lips were parted slightly as the warmth of his breath almost put Hanna into a complete meltdown. Their lips never touching, only the heat from their souls were entangled at this moment. Sam breathing heavily as he made his way to Hanna's neck sent a shallow moan leaking from her mouth. Kissing her with pure hunger and passion it only intensified as he made his way around to her mouth. He kissed her neck, ear, making his way to her eyelid and cheek. Hanna's mouth was open, she was completely intoxicated by his presence.

Going slowly, he seemed to tease her lips which left Hanna longing for him to take her. Sam moved in for the captivating kiss they had both been yearning for. Slow and sensual, open mouthed, his tongue slightly moist. The way their bodies connected was nothing but sheer magic. Frozen within his grip, Hanna was fully engulfed as he immersed himself into her lips. Sam turned Hanna so that her back was towards the bed, he laid her gently upon it without taking his lips from hers. Suddenly Sam disconnected from her, using his fingertips to brush the hair from her face locking contact with her beautiful green eyes.

"Hanna, I want you so much right now, so damn much, but..." The sexual tension was more than they ever expected,

Hanna pulled away from Sam. "I want you as well, my insides feel as they are literally burning but this isn't the time."

"No, it's not, I do however know that when the time is right, it's going to be more than we ever expected. I'm falling in love with you more and more every minute that we spend together, I don't want a heated moment to mess things up."

Hanna looked in Sam's eyes, "I love you for that." Sam didn't want to make a mistake by making love to Hanna with all the changes that were taking place in her life. He knew how complicated she could get and how fast she could get stirred up. He wanted to lead her on so to speak, make her wait for the perfect moment that would leave her in his arms forever and wanting more.

"Stay here, I'm going to take Cloe out for a minute, blow out the candles downstairs and throw a few more logs on the fire." Hanna awe-struck by the glow of the fireplace dancing off the pillows and mirrors, she seemed to be staring into space when she heard the door close. She knew Sam was on his way back up, but he wasn't alone, he had brought Cloe with him. Hanna had taken off her jeans where they laid on the floor beside the bed, she was under the satiny covers, her head and body swallowed by the comfort of the bed. Sam knocked on the door, turning the handle as he walked in. I brought you something. Sam handed Cloe to Hanna to let her comfort her from the cold.

He started to walk back towards the door when Hanna whispered, "Where are you going?"

Sam turned to Hanna, "I thought maybe you would want to sleep with Cloe tonight."

"Well I do, but I also want you here with me too."

Sam was a gentleman, he would never assume his presence was wanted or needed when it came to a woman. He respected Hanna to the fullest, especially after being so incredibly aroused and able to just stop. Sam made his way over to the other side of the room when Hanna asked if he would sleep by the door. She was already in the middle of the bed where she started sliding over as her voice left her lips. Sam smiled knowing she was afraid, he had to remember how she felt being in a new space. He walked back over towards the door, took off his shirt, hanging it upon the doorknob and unzipped his jeans, removing them before crawling into bed. Hanna laid there staring at his almost naked body. He gathered the pillows in just the right position behind his head and pulled Hanna over close to him with one arm. Cloe still intact, he wrapped his arms around Hanna, while she wrapped her legs around his. He kissed her neck ever so gently whispering "Goodnight beautiful."

She clutched his arm tightly, looking out at the moon, "Goodnight Sam." For the first time in Hanna's life she felt as if she belonged, as if she had a purpose, life was giving her a second chance.

8
COINCIDENCE

Hanna had awoken from a sound sleep, still nestled within Sam's grip and Cloe within hers. The cloud coverage was solid over the sun. Hanna could hear the wind blowing through the desolate trees. What she thought was more snow falling was only the drift upon the roof, swirling around in the air before making its final landing. "Looks cold outside," Sam whispered as he pulled the covers up close around Hanna.

"Yeah, this entire trip thing isn't sounding like such a smart idea right now. I honestly hate the cold, it makes me grumpy and miserable,"

Sam snickered under his breath, "And that's different from most days why?"

"Ha-ha, you ass, I need to get dressed, all of my clothes are still in the Inn. I don't even have my toothbrush here so, don't even think about kissing me right now." Hanna climbed out of bed moving Cloe over onto her pillow. The room was warm and toasty from the fireplace, but a whisper of cold air had made its way through the windows. Rushing to put her clothes on to avoid the cold for too long, "Come on, times a wasting, I have phone calls to make, we need to talk to Pete and the Whittles and you need to call Janice."

"Well yes, ma'am," as he propped himself up in bed with his elbow watching Hanna as she slid into her jeans.

"Just remember little miss, if everything falls together today we would leave tomorrow morning early, say five?"

"Oh lord, five! Sure, Pete can sit up front with you and I'll sleep on the way in the back. Oh crap, what about little girl here and picking up Charlie?"

"I'm getting up," Sam could see Hanna was on a roll and until he got out of bed she was not going to stop conversing.

They both had gotten their coats on when Sam backtracked to the fireplace to add logs onto the fire in the living room. Hanna buried Cloe inside of her coat seeing that she had already done her business on the puppy pad somewhere between Hanna putting on her coat, boots and hat. "Little dog, little bladder, I guess I should have spent less time talking and more time moving." They walked outside to feel the cold slap them across the face. Running to the Inn, they looked like something from a horror movie, quickly opening the door, rushing inside to find Mr. and Mrs. Whittle along with Pete having breakfast.

"Lord, close that door, this cold weather is going to be the death of us all." Mrs. Whittle getting up from the table to pour Sam a cup of coffee and Hanna her favorite caramel coffee and hot chocolate. "I have eggs and bacon along with some sausage sitting inside of the oven keeping warm." Hanna slipped off her boots before unzipping her coat." "Oh, honey, what do you have there," Mrs. Whittle reaching over to Hanna's coat pulling Cloe out and into her arms.

"This is Cloe, she was a special gift from Sam last night."

"Well she is absolutely adorable, come here my little munchkin." Mrs. Whittle had sat back down holding Cloe in her arms as if she were holding a newborn child.

"Pete, Mr. and Mrs. Whittle, I have a question and a favor." Everyone seemed to look up from the table at once. Next week we are going to be busy here at the Inn actually, from Wednesday on and since Hanna and Pete," Sam, nodding his head Pete's direction, "Well, will be staying with us from here on out it's important that we are able to get to their places and gather their belongings. Mr. and Mrs. Whittle, if it would not be too much to ask would you mind staying here to watch over the Inn and make any reservations that may come in?" They looked at each other shrugging their shoulders before turning to Sam. "I would, of course, pay you for your time here as well, and throw in a puppy to watch over as well?" Sam knew he was asking what seemed to be a lot with the concerned look that he had upon his face.

"Now Sam, we could never tell you no. Of course, we will stay. Why don't you make a few short lists of things you need done as well and me and the Mr. will do what we can."

Sam looked up with a smile, "Two days tops is all we will be gone, we will leave around five tomorrow morning and be back the following day pretty early."

"Then it's settled," Pete taking a sip from his coffee, "One more day closer to the beginning of a new life." Hanna and Pete both took this opportunity to pack an overnight bag for the trip, Sam would follow suit but not before making one last call to Janice over at the shelter, as he had promised to Hanna. He explained about them wanting to adopt Charlie for a companion to Pete when they weren't around, not to mention it would give Cloe a playmate. He had really wanted to get Charlie over to the Inn but with the impending trip he couldn't figure out how not to overwhelm the Whittles.

Hanna grunting as she stumbled down the steps. "Hanna, are you bringing the kitchen sink with you?" Sam laughing as he held Cloe in his arms.
"No, no, I'm moving all of my things over to our home and then I'm going to go ahead and clean the suite. I want it ready so that when we get back I can decorate it for the upcoming guests."

"Have I told you how beautiful you are today?" Hanna walking past Sam with a smug look on her face.

"Nope, not today." Hanna rushed over to the carriage house to get her things put away before taking a quick shower to freshen up. She had an uneasy feeling, the first since being at the Inn. Things seemed to get a bit blurry, her heart racing. Her body, hot and freezing at the same time. Hanna caught herself yelling for Sam, but no one was nearby to hear her. Her medicine bottle was in her purse over at the Inn, she was feeling an intense sense of doom, something unstoppable was about to occur and she was alone. Managing to get dressed, she held on tight to the handrail making her way down the stairs. In the middle of all the excitement, she lost her balance falling half a flight of stairs, knocking her head on the floor below. Hanna was screaming and crying that she didn't want to die when it was Cloe that could hear Hanna from inside the Inn.

"Cloe, what are you doing?" Cloe had jumped out of Sam's arms and ran to the kitchen door where she was whimpering and scratching aggressively. "Do you need to go potty?" Sam opened the door, Cloe darted out in a full run to the carriage house. "Cloe, where are you going?" Sam ran out of the Inn leaving the door wide open running after Cloe. She was sitting at the door looking up at Sam barking, but this wasn't her normal bark, this was more of an alarming bark.

"Hanna," Sam swung the door open where he saw her laying at the bottom of the stairs. "Oh my God, Pete, Pete!" Sam yelled at the top of his voice, enough to gather Pete's attention from inside the kitchen. He ran to Sam's voice to find him slumped over top of Hanna. "Help me get her up and onto the couch, close the door so that Cloe doesn't get out!"

Hanna was awake, never losing consciousness. Her body was soaked with sweat as she laid on the couch trembling. Sam ran back over to the Inn to grab his medical bag when he noticed Hanna's purse, "Her meds," he grabbed it throwing it over his shoulder as well, as he ran back to the carriage house. Mr. and Mrs. Whittle were in the kitchen at the time preparing a gourmet lunch when they could not help but notice all the excitement and followed Sam over.

"Hanna darling," Mrs. Whittle was full of emotion as she saw her lay on the couch with a look of sheer panic on her face. Sam quickly ran to her side, placing a cuff on her arm as he spoke to her in a calm manner.

"I'm cold," Hanna managed to get out of her chilling voice.

"All right let's get this blanket on you, Pete, do you mind covering her up for me and getting her medication bottle out of her purse, it's the one that begins with an A." Pete took the blanket from the couch and tucked it around Hanna as she focused on Sam's face. Pete handed Sam one of the pills from Hanna's prescription. "Pete, why don't you give me two, I need to get this under control for her."

Hanna started to calm down after about twenty minutes, but not before completely losing her mind. Her heart rate started to slow, sweating had seized, and the trembling had calmed to a mild shiver. "Hanna, what happened? Does anything hurt?" Sam was checking her over once again now that she was off the floor.

"I don't know, I felt a panic attack coming on, I realized I didn't have my medication, phone, nothing. I completely let it take over me, not that I know how to stop them from happening. But it was fast, intense, I thought I was going to die before I could reach you, I only fell down the stairs because I missed a step." Hanna lay on the couch, looking up into Sam's eyes. "I thought I was going to die alone, thought that was it." Sam sat Hanna up on the couch just enough to squeeze underneath her and hold her in his arms. His hand lightly rubbing the top of her arm, to take her brain from the attack and onto his touch.

Pete watched as the concerned look on Sam's face lessened. "Well, that's it then." Sam looked up at Pete,

"What's what?" "Hanna is all of your stuff that you need from your apartment boxed and ready to go?"

"Um, I think so from the calls I made, Sara is keeping all of my furniture, she boxed all of my personal belongings along with my closet."

"Why don't you give them a call when you settle down, be sure and give me your address out there. I think it's best you stay put, Sam if it's ok I would like to take your truck and Mr. Whittle, I would love the company if the Mrs. wouldn't mind you taking a short trip with me."

"I can't let you do that, it's my belongings, you have your own to worry about." Hanna leaning her head up from Sam's chest.

"Nonsense, we just saw you go down from an attack, I know those things wipe people out, Sam you can back me on this one. You need your rest, Sam needs to stay put with you. Mrs. Whittle can stay in your guest room tonight or you both can spend one last night in the Lilac Room before you work your Christmas magic in there, letting Mrs. Whittle stay comfy in her quarters."

Hanna leaned back into Sam's arms with a soft smile upon her face as Sam spoke. "Take what you need to Pete, I've got a gas card just above the visor, the code is 3456, use it. Are you sure you don't want to just postpone a day or two? We can go with you."

"Nonsense, it makes better sense anyway for only one of us to go."

Sam marched up the stairs to collect a change of clothes along with Hanna's night clothes and overnight bag. Skipping back down where Pete held out his hands to take all of Hanna's things. Mrs. Whittle was holding on tight to Cloe and Sam leaned over to help Hanna up from the couch. "What are we doing Sam?"

"Well ladybug, we are going to spend one last night in the lilac room to keep Mrs. Whittle company tomorrow night while the guys are gone." Looking over to Mrs. Whittle, "You girls can discuss how you want to decorate and get a jump start on it tomorrow." They all scurried their way back over to the Inn where Sam took Hanna up to her old room.

"I really thought I was going to die." Hanna looked up at Sam with such a concerned look on her face.

"But you didn't, you have had a lot going on the past week, even though you have been having what seems to be a good time, a lot in your life has changed. It's no wonder it happened, but I promise you, you're ok." Hanna was exhausted from her episode, combined with her medications. Head pounding, Sam tucked her into bed and turned on the fireplace.

"This is what I was talking about from the beginning," Hanna whispered as she closed her eyes.

"What are you talking about?"

"It's not right for you and everyone else to have to deal with me and my issues, it's not welcoming for anyone to take on my problems."

"Nonsense, you're where you're supposed to be, now close your eyes, I'll be right here." Sam sat quietly with her till she faded off to sleep.

Mrs. Whittle was busy in the kitchen with Cloe right by her feet. "She doing ok?" Pete standing in the doorway as Sam walked by.

"Yeah, she's doing much better, finally drifted off to sleep, she's had a lot going on the past week with all the new changes, the snowstorm, feeling stuck."

"Good thing we weren't on that train today, it's sort of coincidental that we were here, by the way, I could not help but hear our little ladybug talking about her issues becoming ours, I don't think she's ever had people to just take care of her and listen."

"Pete, there's nothing coincidental about it, my mom always taught me that nothing is coincidental, God puts us where we are supposed to be when we are needed."

"You might be right on that one, I can't imagine what she would have done had she gone into a full-blown attack like on the drive back home or on the train to her parents."

"Exactly, the man upstairs knew, he put us all where we needed to be today." Pete looked down at his coffee,

"Don't let her think for a second that we don't want her here, I don't care if she comes down loopy on her meds dancing in her undies, we will take care of her always." Sam picked up Hanna's clothes and overnight bag, shaking his head with a smile as he headed back up to the Lilac room, but not before letting Mrs. Whittle know he would return to get little Cloe.

"Not a chance," Mrs. Whittle turned to Sam. "I'm finishing up some chocolate chip cookies for the guys, made just enough to bring you up a plate as well with some hot chocolate, I'll have the Mr. bring Cloe up when I'm ready, I can't remember the last time I was filled with such contentment with a little rag muffin by my side." Mrs. Whittle turned back around towards the oven before igniting the flame to boil the water. Sam, with a warm smile on his face, continued his walk back up to Hannah.

Upon Sam's return, he quietly opened the door not to wake Hannah. He carefully laid her belongings down onto the floor hanging her clothes in the bathroom. Hannah was awake, but she laid there quietly, afraid to turn over. She had awakened from a bizarre dream. Only it didn't feel like a dream and although there was nothing scary about it, it left her with a heightened feeling of anxiety. Sam walked over towards the winged back chair where he had planned to sit for a few and watch over Hannah when he heard her voice. "It's you?"

Sam turned towards Hannah, "Of course it's me, who were you expecting?"

"I don't know, I had the weirdest dream that I was lying in bed and when I rolled over there was this little boy, maybe 7 or 8 just staring at me, he made a face and raspberries at me before he turned around and walked through the door." Pointing, afraid to look. Hannah knew she sounded crazy, "Maybe I should go get my head checked out today, make sure I didn't end up with a concussion or something from my fall yesterday."

Sam moved over to Hannah on the bed and sat down beside her, he brushed the hair away from her face ever so slightly, "What did the little boy look like?"

"What does that matter, don't you see, I have some sort of trauma going on here?"

"I really don't think so, but first just explain to me in detail what he looked like and we can go from there."

"All right, but you really need to listen to how I'm feeling." Sam shook his head with sincere interest. "Like I said, he was maybe seven or eight, maybe younger, I'm just not sure. He was wearing a little sailor outfit and had blonde hair and blue eyes, but it wasn't like you and I sitting here right now, he didn't seem real. He was lying beside me right here." Hannah turned her body slightly to show Sam that the image was where he would be lying if he had been in bed with her. "He went from watching me sleep with a smile on his face to standing beside the bed. I never saw him get up, the next thing I know he is standing by the door blowing raspberries at me and then vanished through the door." Sam knew whom Hannah was speaking of but wasn't sure how to explain this to her just yet. With the state of mind that Hannah had been in, he really didn't want to shake her any more than what she was already.

"Well you're not expressing anything that I am alarmed about now, but if you want we can go down to the Doc and let him look at you. I really think your fine, is anything hurting this morning?"

Hannah sat up in bed, no not really, grabbing her left shoulder and neck. 'Uncomfortable yes but hurting not really." A knock came to the door.

Christmas in Hunter's Grove

9
IF BY CHANCE

"Good morning Hannah dear, did you sleep well?" Mrs. Whittle strolled her way into the room placing the cookies and hot chocolate upon the table. Mr. Whittle followed behind with Cloe.

"Cloe, I've missed you," Hannah reached her arms out to take her from Mr. Whittle.

"The misses has taken fondly of her, as you can see. may have to visit Janice for a little pip squeak of our own."

Hannah looked up at Mr. Whittle, "She's been a blessing, that's for sure."

"Pete and I are going to start packing our overnight bags for tomorrow morning. You two still plan on staying here at the Inn with the Misses?"

"Yes sir, she won't be alone." Hanna looked over to Mrs. Whittle with a smile on her face.

"Well good, we're going to head back downstairs so she can help me pick out my clothes, not like I can't do it myself." Mr. Whittle grumbling to himself. He was a funny man, stern in his day but now you could tell he just went with the flow of life.

"Why don't you get yourself together Hannah, I'll run you down to Doc's and we can sneak away to go look at the dogs. While Pete and Mr. Whittle are out of town it might be the perfect time for us to pick out the Inn's new member."

Hannah perked up, that sounds great, but will you stay here in the room while I get ready?"

"I can, but what for?"

"I just feel weird still, don't want to see any more people that aren't really here." Sam sat down on the bed, turned on the television and assured Hannah he would be right there. Hannah scurried to get ready, she was excited for the new day but was still concerned over what she thought she had seen.

"Hey Pete, are you ready for tomorrow?" Sam and Hannah entered the kitchen.

"Look at you, you're looking a lot better than yesterday." Pete looking up from his coffee to notice Hannah had her color back and was just as spunky as ever.

"Yeah, besides seeing things and my shoulder I'm feeling pretty good today."

"Seeing things?" Mrs. Whittle spoke up. Sam scurried to speak before Hanna,

"Yeah, nothing to be concerned with, going to take Hanna over to see Doc, just to be sure she's ok. Do any of you need anything while we're gone?"

"Nope, all good here." Mrs. Whittle sat down at the kitchen table with the men snacking on leftover pieces of cookie.

"OK, we will be gone a couple of hours, I need to get a few errands done and place an order for some fresh flowers before our guests arrive. We've got two rooms left to decorate and I think we are all set and back in business." Sam helped Hanna with her coat and slipped on his flannel.

"There were a couple of messages on the phone, I'll take care of returning those while you're gone." Pete stood from the table pouring another cup of coffee.

Hanna looked over to Mrs. Whittle. "Mrs. Whittle?"

"Yes dear."

"Would you mind keeping Cloe company while we're out, she's grown quite fond of you and would hate to leave her in the room alone."

Mrs. Whittle stood from the table with a smile, holding out her arms as she made kissing sounds towards Cloe. "Of course, she can even be my bed partner while the Mr. is gone if that's all right." Hanna leaned over and kissed Mrs. Whittle on the cheek, handed Cloe over into her arms.

"That would be more than fine, I'm sure she would like to have a sleepover with her grandma." Mrs. Whittle could not help but tear up as she looked into Cloe's little black eyes.

"Well, of course, she knows she's in good hands. Now you two scurry on."

Hanna and Sam slipped out the back door, leaving Cloe in good care with Mrs. Whittle. On their way to the doctors, Sam spoke up. "Hanna, I don't think there is anything really wrong with you. It's an old house with many who have come and gone from long ago past."

"What do you mean?" Hanna looking up at Sam with an inquisitive look upon her face. "I mean there have been tales of the Inn for many years of people seeing spirits of the past amongst the walls. No one has ever been harmed, most everyone speaks of a passive feeling as if Guardian Angels are watching over them."

"Are you telling me I saw a ghost?"

"By remote chance, you expressed information about the same little boy who has been seen by many. My mom claims to have even seen him, my dad and I never witnessed any of it, but there's more." Hanna was inquisitive to what Sam had to say. "Like I said, it's an old house and a lot of our guests have had many stories that they have shared around the breakfast table.

"Like...," Hanna's eyes were wide with wonder, yearning for more information where Sam was hesitant to tell her all that he and his parents had heard.

"I just think that maybe we should just be patient, see what else you come across and not listen to a bunch of stories."

"Sam, if you think for a second I am going to be running an Inn where I have to tiptoe around to see what else comes out of the corners of that house, you're crazy. I know I'm nuts, that's been confirmed, but not knowing is worse than knowing for me. I think I've been tolerant to not know about the little sailor boy and what he was up to. I was scared shitless." She turned her head looking out the window. "No need to take me to see the Doc, I'm obviously fine, just seeing a little mean ass ghost boy." Sam clenched his lips together trying not to laugh, holding it in with his finger covering his mouth and elbow on the truck's door.

"You're sure, no Doc?"

"I have bad headaches that come and go, hear beeping noises in my head and now, seeing a little ghost boy,"

Hanna glared over at Sam, "Well then that's out of the way, ready to go see some pups?" Hanna shook her head looking back out the window as they traveled down the road to meet back up with Janice.

As they pulled up in front of the Animal Shelter Sam observed Janice outside trying to shovel her walk. He grabbed his spare coat from the back seat and jumped out to help but not before helping Hanna out of the truck and inside the shelter. "Hey Janice, we're here to find another pup, this one is going to be for the Inn, Pete's dog really, he's my new part-time chef and manager. I'll let Hanna fill you in, give me that shovel. I'll finish up here and you all can pick out the perfect pup for Pete."

Hanna and Janice looked at each other before looking at Sam, Hanna shrugged her shoulders. "That man I swear, I want to kill him one minute and kiss him the next." Janice laughed as she opened the gate that leads down the hall.

"Well come along let's see if we can find a match for Pete." Hanna followed behind where she entered the puppy retreat. "Now let's see, tell me a little about Pete," Janice pulled her book out to look over all the characteristics of the pups. First, we need to see which ones a good fit for the Inn and its visitors.

"Well we were looking at Charlie in the book, I know Sam called you yesterday about him, is he still available?"

"I thought about him, he really needs a more one on one with the owner, that type of breed doesn't like to be left alone and require a lot of attention. He would be more suited for a single person or older couple that doesn't travel a lot."

"That's a shame, he was just adorable, well Pete is in his mid-60's, he was in the military for years before becoming a train conductor."

"Train conductor?"

"Yes, he said after being in the military he could not stand being in just one place after his wife died some time ago and he wanted to be able to travel, that his home wasn't home any longer after she passed." Janice looked at Hanna with sadness in her eyes.

"Oh, don't feel sorry for him, he doesn't, it was just a way for him to rebuild, so he sold their house, moved into a tiny one-bedroom apartment and saw parts of the states that we could only dream of. He's happy, loving, caring yet, that old Medic in him peeks out occasionally. He's firm, yet gentle. He's about six feet, takes care of himself very well, I would have never known his age had he not told me."

"Well, it seems as if Sam not only brought one new amazing person to this town but two." Hanna smiled at Janice as she sat on the floor to visit with the pups.

"Well, it looks like I have about four that would be a good fit for our old Marine." Janice walked amongst the pups picking up the ones that may not be a good fit and placed them inside of their baby gate. The others were left out to see how they acted around Hanna without the rest of them running around in the mix. "Well this is Daniel, he's a Miniature Schnauzer, loving, loyal, great with kids and families but can catch an attitude from time to time. This is Larry, he's a labradoodle. Affectionate, loyal, has that fatherly look about him, great family dog as well. Next, we have Barney, he's a beagle mix, he's very loving and great with small children. Only one problem, I haven't been able to get that bark under control yet. That might be a bit of a problem at the Inn. Oh and last we have Chance, He's a Border Collie, they are not great dogs to be cooped up, they need their exercise but it sounds like Chance would be a part of the Inn so teaching him small tasks like walking up the stairs with the guests, to just having the run of the place would be nice, not to mention you said how Pete still seems to be in good shape, it would be easy to play catch with him daily outside or just take him for a walk. Chance has the brains of all the pups here, it's in his nature. He could be taught multiple tasks and is a great family dog." Hanna looked around at the puppies, she wanted to take every one of them but knew they had only come here for one more.

"Janice, what happens to the pups that don't get adopted?" "Well, that doesn't really ever happen. Most of them are gone within three months or so, some a little longer, but not to worry they would never be harmed. They are all a part of my family, I have no kids, husband, it's just me and them."

Janice rubbing Larry's belly as she and Hanna finished their conversation. "Then it's settled, I think Chance would be a great addition to the Inn. I know Pete will just love him, not to mention teaching him new tricks and since we've opened the attic rooms Pete now has the whole front side with a gated balcony and all. I think they are a perfect fit and a fit for the Inn."

"Well ok, let's go start the paperwork and get all of that out of the way."

Sam had finished the walkway and had just walked in at the end of Janice and Hanna's conversation. "Did we find a winner for Pete?"

"I think so, he's beautiful, well handsome. His name is Chance, he's a border collie, great with kids and family, very intelligent, loves to learn and to get exercise and not much of a barker."

"Chance? Janice, can I go back and see him?" Janice nodding her head, she gathered the papers Sam would need to sign and took them back to the pup room.

"He's right there," Hanna pointing out the black and white fluff ball. He will only get to be about thirty pounds, but he's going to be energetic."

"Yes, he will be, but I think with him having full run of the Inn until he goes up with Pete at night and walks daily or just throwing him a ball from the front porch a couple times a day will be fine." Janice stood at the counter.

"Chance huh, he sure is fluffy," Sam knelt over to pick him up, Chance licking him in his face whimpering with excitement. "Let's sign the papers, I think he will be amazing for the Inn, for us and for Pete." Janice and Sam sat down and started filling out the paperwork. Hanna talking a mile a minute to the newest edition about meeting Cloe and the life he would have at the Inn. This put a warm smile on Sam's face as he signed the last page of the adoption paperwork. "Well we can't take him today, Pete is still there. We can come back bright and early when Janice opens up and pick up the little fur ball in the morning."

Hanna placed Chance back down onto the floor amongst the rest of the pups, nodding her head in agreement with a smile as big as the ocean upon her face. "Oh, by the way," Sam looking over to Hanna, "We have a hundred-dollar credit with Janice on file, do you want to pick out some things for the dogs while we're here?"

"Yes, love to." Hanna headed back up front to the store part of the shelter. Besides the Vet in town, Janice was the only other person who sold items for domestic animals, she also had a rather lavish boutique for her furry little clients. "Is this a crochet blanket, I love it!" It was made up of small stripes of different shades of pinks and white.

166

"I make those in my spare time, they are a pretty big seller. It's what helps to keep the shelter program going. I take the money from the blankets, minus my expenses for the yarn and can purchase all the dog food that they need at my cost. Doc McFarland takes care of five to seven pups a month for me with their shots, neutering/spaying along with the well visits. The community donates old blankets, toys, treats, it works great. Not to mention I have a couple of sponsors who donate a sizeable check every year that keeps the electric and water going."

"Oh Sam, we need to take some of the blankets to the Inn to sell, they might not work for adults but could be used as lap blankets, children's blankets or for their furry family members. And, with me handling the event planning we could showcase a couple of them, Janice if you could make a couple large ones to put into our wedding and anniversary packages, we could give you the profit from them to help the shelter out."

Sam smiling, watching the excitement in Hanna's eyes. "She hasn't even worked her first day yet and already coming up with amazing ideas."

"Those ideas will bring you much success, Sam." Janice spoke as she took a few of her blankets from the top shelf, handing them gently down to

Hanna. Hanna bought two blankets, one for each of the dogs, along with dog food, play toys and treats.

"Oh, I almost forgot," Hanna reached out beside her to grab a package of hair bows for little Ms. Cloe along with a red and white fur-trimmed coat to help keep her warm outside.

"Is that all?" Sam only knew to shake his head around her and either laugh or smile for Hanna was full of excitement when she was in her comfort zone. He loved watching that sparkle in her eyes with every facial expression she made.

"Yes, that is all." Laying the rest of the items up on the counter for Janice to ring up.

"All right Sam, the total is $75.00 for the adoption and then all of the goodies come out to be $84.63, so you still have a credit on your account."

"No, keep the change, buy something for the pups." Sam gathered the bags of dog food in his arms and Hanna reached over for the bag of goodies and blankets for her to showcase at the Inn.

"I can't wait to get this stuff set up for our guests to see, we will be back in the morning to pick up Chance."

Sam gave Janice a nod, see ya in the morning, Janice." She opened the door to help Sam and Hanna out, "Will see you tomorrow!" Janice closed the door behind them and watched as they pulled out and onto the street.

"Chance, what a perfect name and a perfect dog for the Inn and Pete." Hanna looked over at Sam, "Yes it was by Chance that fate brought us to your town, it was by chance that you had rooms available and by chance that we all took to one another. It's not like we had made advanced plans to ever stop here and through chance or fate, the storm brought us all to you."

For the first time since Hanna's arrival at the Inn, Sam knew in his heart that this was all meant to be. He knew it was fate that brought Pete and Hanna to him a few days ago, in the middle of what became a very large blizzard. He looked up at the sky and gave a wink. He felt somehow his mom, dad, God, someone had something to do with them meeting by chance.

Christmas in Hunter's Grove

10
JUST BREATHE

Hanna and Sam took it slow walking back to the Inn. Grasping the doorknob Hanna could hardly contain her excitement and wanted to tell Mrs. Whittle so badly about the new addition but knew to keep it a secret until morning. "Hi everyone!" Hanna full of cheer and anticipation. She slid up to the Lilac room almost immediately with Cloe in hand to try on her dress and hair bow. Like a whirlwind, she was in and up.

"Lord, that girl has some energy today." Mrs. Whittle spoke while working on some of her recipes at the kitchen table. "I'm taking it that her noggin is still intact?" Mr. Whittle sitting beside the misses broke out in laughter.

"Yeah, she's intact all right. We went shopping for Cloe and obviously, she couldn't wait to go get her all dressed up".

"Dressed up?" Mrs. Whittle looked up at Sam.

"Yes ma'am, they make all kinds of clothing for these little four-legged friends these days. I'm actually shocked she only picked out one outfit, I was sure I was coming home with a mini closet to go with the mini dog." Mr. Whittle just sat there laughing in amusement.

"I wish you laughed this much at home." Mrs. Whittle glanced over to the Mr. Sam glanced over to the Whittles,

"Well, I can honestly say I'm for one going to miss this when you both go back to the store. It's been great having everyone around, it hasn't felt like home in such a long time. The walls of this place are finally filled with love again."

"Well Sam," Mr. Whittle spoke up, "Me and the misses, well we've have been doing a lot of talking. We had an investor interested in the old place a couple of months back, was going to pay us a pretty lousy penny, but with all the work that needs to be done to the place and not knowing where we would go since he wouldn't allow us to stay in our apartment." Mr. Whittle let out a deep sigh. Sam slowly pulled out a chair at the table to sit and listen to what Mr. Whittle had to say. "Do you really need both the rooms upstairs for a housekeeper and the supplies? Do you think the supplies could be moved over to the storage room leaving a large living area there?"

"You want to stay?" Sam was shocked. Mrs. Whittle looked up from her recipes,

"Well we had thought since there was an elevator I would no longer have to climb a set of steps, it's been bad on my knees. The housekeeper's bedroom is about the same size as what we have now and would work well for us. We thought maybe the door in between the housekeeping bedroom and linen room could be opened and made into a nice size living room, it has a full bath already, a fireplace, a back balcony and all to sit and watch the families who come and stay here. It's so much nicer and roomier than what we have now. We would want to pay you rent, but could also help out around here with breakfast for maybe a cheaper rent?"

Sam for such a strong man about broke down into tears. Everything he had been missing in his life for so long was becoming a reality. He could not believe by keeping the Inn that he would become the richest man in the world. Not by money, but by respect and love. "Oh Mr. and Mrs. Whittle, are you sure? You were mom and pop's dearest friends, I would love nothing more than to have you here. We would need to move things around upstairs a bit and move the washer and dryer possibly into a smaller room that I could build in the storage wing, but as far as moving the shelving units and all, that could easily be done. I would need to have the balcony inspected and fix whatever may be wrong with it. It's been blocked for so long by all the housekeeping equipment, it hasn't been used in years."

Mrs. Whittle's eyes swelled with tears, her prayers had been answered as well, but in a different way. She and the Mr. were never able to have their own children, life had been quiet with only each other month after month, year after year. The Inn had brought life back to their souls. They had a sense of belonging and being wanted.

"It's settled, Mr. Whittle when you get back with Pete we will sit down and figure out when the right time will be to start on this project, you can also call the investor today and see if he is still interested. If he is, set up a meeting next week, the beginning if possible and I'll sit in on it with you both. I just want to be sure you're getting a fair deal with no nonsense."

Mr. Whittle went to shake Sam's hand when Hanna stumbled upon what felt an intense situation. "Is everything all right?"

"Couldn't be better dear." Mrs. Whittle wiping tears of happiness from her cheek.

"Well if you both don't mind I would like to take Hanna out on a proper date tonight. Would you mind if Cloe slept in your room, I would be sure to bring her pillow, food and water bowl down? Don't worry, this won't happen often. Just felt like it was time she was treated for a night out before she starts her new job on Monday." Sam took Hanna's hand smiling down at her.

Mrs. Whittle lit with excitement, "Yes of course. I will babysit anytime and no need for a pillow, little Cloe will sleep either with us or on my quilt beside the fireplace." Mrs. Whittle patting her hands together with excitement. Hanna saw that life was not only breathing again with the living but within the walls of the old Victorian as well.

Sam had sent Hanna upstairs allowing her the time she needed to get ready for their evening on the town. He quietly escaped to the back room to call one of his favorite wineries to see if it would be possible for them to clear off a couple of chairs outback that overlooked the town of Hunters Grove. He asked the owner if they could set up a table between the chairs and lite the fire pit to keep them warm. He also stated that he wanted to let Hanna do a wine tasting inside to kind of throw her off from the dinner he had planned just outside on the back deck. The owner was more than excited to help plan this special evening for Sam. He had always been a great customer, purchasing all his wine orders through them for his guests and recommending their establishment to all of them as well.

Hanna was flying through her suitcase trying to figure out the right combination for a winter date night. Not knowing if they would be inside or walking around outdoors one thing was for sure, she hated to be cold. She managed to take the rollers out of her hair after applying her makeup. She found a light gray thermal long sleeve that she put on before diving into her comfy cream-colored long sweater. Hanna grabbed her charcoal infinity scarf from the bottom of her bag and placed it over her head and around her neck, brushed out her hair, but not before placing her large button style gold earrings upon her ears. She threw on her favorite skinny jeans and then layered up with a pair of her gray thermal sloth socks, she pulled her wool lined boots up on her legs before placing her smoky topaz and gold bracelet on her wrist. Dabbing her sheer pink lip-gloss upon her lips, she was ready for whatever may be in store.

Hanna walked down the stairs with gloves in hand, stopping in front of an old antique mirror that hung on the wall. "Why am I so nervous? Snap out of it Hanna, it's not like you haven't had your first kiss." Hanna had always been hard on herself, not knowing where it ever came from, she just always wanted to look as perfect as she could be before leaving the house. With Sam, she never wanted to look unkempt, although that had happened daily since her arrival. A reminder of her outer beauty to go with her inner is what she was after this night. "What the hell?" Hanna let out a scream. Sam ran towards the stairs to see Hanna just sitting there.

"What's wrong, are you ok?" Sam could not take his eyes off Hanna, she was simply beautiful.

"Yes, just startled is all. That little sailor boy again, I saw myself laying in a bed with him holding my hand. Then he blew me a kiss and all I could hear was a loud repetitive beeping sound, repeatedly."

Sam just smiled, "Well obviously he thinks you're as beautiful as I do."

Hanna fidgeting with her scarf, "Funny, why does he do that, scare me? I mean I don't feel threatened by him in the least, he just freaks me out with this appearing like a puff of air in front of me."

"Like I said, he seems to like you, he's not going to harm you, maybe you remind him of his mother or sister or maybe you're just new to him and he thinks you're adorable. Either way, let's keep this little guy to ourselves. I certainly don't want to scare the Whittles right now."

"Deal, good night little guy, see you tomorrow." Hanna whispered to her obvious new little friend. She felt as if she was losing her mind at this point, not only seeing spirits but now talking to them.

Sam helped Hanna up from the staircase, "You really are beautiful tonight. Are you ready for a night out on the town?" Before Hanna could answer, Sam dropped Hanna's hand and told her to stand by the front door that he would be right back.

The masculine charms of the doorbell rang through the first floor. "Sam!" Hanna called out, unknowing if they were expecting any guests or neighbors. With no response, Hanna gently gripped the doorknob, opening the door to a pleasant surprise.

"Good evening ma'am, your chariot awaits." Sam had made his way around to the front walk, his truck sitting idle in the driveway. He held out his hand to take Hanna's and handed her a single white rose with the other. "Just breathe," Sam whispered into Hanna's ear. He could see the nervousness in those vast green eyes of hers. Her first real date, first time truly out, inside of the town. She stepped off the landing and down the sidewalk as Sam opened the door helping her up inside of the warmth.

They made their way down the drive and into town. Taking the winding roads slowly, although the destination was less than two miles away, Sam had taken an alternative route for Hanna to take in the magic of Christmas. Lights sparkled against the snow giving off the perfect gleam of light, the clean crisp air spoke of winter's bliss. The icicles dangled from the lights that streamed across Main Street. The old lantern style street lights, people dressed in their winters best, it all set the stage for such a mystical atmosphere. Sam drove up the hill through the county roads to this beautiful winery, tucked away on the side of the mountain's ridge. "Were here!" Hanna expelled as Sam placed the truck in park, turning off the ignition to quickly open his door and jump over to open Hanna's.

"Yes, we are, hope you're hungry." They stepped swiftly to the front door, for leaving the warmth of the truck sent a chill to Hanna's body.

"Oh, my goodness, what a quaint café," as a small cat made its way over to Hanna.

"Please let me help you with your coat," Sam helped Hanna as she got more comfortable in her setting, placing their coats upon the hooks beside the entryway. He took her hand and led her over to a quiet corner in the café where there was a beautiful candlelight centerpiece illuminating the table. The waitress had made her way over to the table where Sam spoke up that they would love to have a menu and that they would be doing two separate flight tastings.

"What is a flight, Sam?" Hanna a bit confused about his wording.

"It's a wine tasting that is served on a wooden long plate that includes four different wines of your choice. Sip slowly, they give you four ounces per glass here."

"Oh, that sounds great, I've never been anywhere that does that." Sam looked over the menu,

"Are you in the mood for pizza, spaghetti?" Hanna stopped him quickly, "Pizza, we have not had just a fun dinner since I arrived, fun meaning simple, no silverware, just our hands."

"Pizza it is,"

"Are you ready to order?"

"Yes," Sam rubbing his hands together. "We would like the large homemade brick oven pizza with pepperoni and pineapples."

"That's an interesting choice, I like it." Hanna looked up at Sam and then over to the waitress with a smile.

"Let's go up to the bar so that you can look over the wines they have here. I know something is going to pop out at you but believe me they all have their own identity." They both sat at the same time, Sam remembering that he needed to introduce himself to the bartender so that she would know he and Hanna were there. The surprise had to be subtle, Hanna seemed to catch on to most things and since everything was being sat up behind them outside it made for the perfect spot over the next twenty minutes or so. Hanna was scrolling through the wine list, knowing that the sweeter the better, she was attempting to make a wise choice. "Well, why we are choosing, excuse Ms. While we're working on our wine choice could we order the cheese, olive oil, and bread platter to go with it?"

The bartender making eye contact with Sam, "Sure, I'll get that right in and just let me know when you're ready with your selections."

"Humm, I think I'm going to try the American Concord sweet red, the Niagara, the American Cranberry and the American Fredonia, what about you?"

Sam looked over the list one last time before making his selections. "Ok, why don't I get the Red Raspberry, the Ohio Apple, Rhubarb and the Blackberry? I think this way we have covered them all or at least most of them."

"That sounds great, we can taste eight of them at least." Hanna was excited, wine tasting was one of her favorite things to do during the summer months. It was odd doing it during the snow, yet a blessing they were able to leave the Inn. She was surprised at how diverse wineries could have such an amazingly distinct flavor all their own. Sam placed their flight orders and while the server was preparing them their cheese tray had been delivered. Smelling each glass before swirling the magical potion in their mouths, they tried each receiving the familiar with the sweetest, ones with a hint of tartness to the captivating flavors of honeydew, apples, raspberries and of course grapes. "This winery really does have a unique grasp on their winemaking." Hanna was enjoying each sip with the cheese platter. All the wines were perfect, the rhubarb was pleasantly sweet with just a hint of the rhubarb to follow. "Oh lord, the Cranberry, It's like Thanksgiving in a bottle." Hanna sat there sipping on the smoothness. "I have to have to purchase a bottle or two for Thanksgiving because it's exactly what it tastes like."

Sam was so intrigued by how Hanna used her words. "It tastes like Thanksgiving?" Sam laughing as he took another bite of the bread and olive oil.

"Yes, cranberry chutney, have you never had it?"

"No, I don't believe I ever have."

"Well, I'm telling you it's Thanksgiving in a bottle. "Oh, and the Fredonia, this is exquisite, yes it's a grapy wine, but I don't know, it's just got such a unique flavor, like nothing I've tasted. Lord, do you realize that a glass of wine is five ounces, we've almost had four glasses of wine each." Hanna was in delight being able to try so many different tastes that exhausted her taste buds. Not to mention being able to enjoy herself with real food instead of the bread bullets, as she liked to call them. The tasting was over, and she had indeed decided to purchase two of the Cranberry for Thanksgiving, one of the Fredonia and a bottle of the Niagara for Sam.

"Wow, would you look at it out there." Sam touched Hanna on her shoulder in a motion to turn around to see what lay behind her. "Wow, is that a firepit lit up out there?"

"Yep," Sam got up from the tasting paying the server for her time and purchases for the evening. He went to the door to retrieve their coats. Sliding his on, he helped Hanna with hers and even skimmed around to her front, buttoning each button while gazing into her eyes. "I have a surprise for you, come on."

"Sam, I hate the cold, what are we doing?"

"Trust me, you will keep warm, let's go."

"Oh my God."

"What? Just breathe." Sam had ahold of Hanna's hand leading her over to the two comfortable chairs in sight with a lower scale bistro table that sat in between. Right in front was a roaring fire that quickly captivated Hanna. "Dinner is served." The poor waiter had on his coat and gloves to bring out their pizza, he also took information from the server and grabbed what was left of the Riesling since it paired nicely with the Hawaiian side of the pizza.

"Were eating out here!" Hanna was full of smiles and laughter in her voice.

"Why of course, best views around." They sat there in entertaining conversation of how the days had been leading up to this point. They spoke of ideas for the Inn and what it was going to be like having everyone there with them. They spoke of what might go bump in the night to Cloe and Chance. The night seemed to slip by for they only had the place for a couple of hours. Lost in conversation and within each other Sam took Hanna once again by the hand as dinner was finished. "I want you to see this." Walking down on the deck, Sam stood behind Hanna with his arms wrapped around her tight. The town below glowed in the most mystical of ways. It's as if for that moment, Hanna envisioned she was on Santa's sleigh looking down at the town with the same views Santa would have upon arriving amongst the rooftops. In an instant music filled the air and echoed across the mountain. Sam took Hanna by the hand. "I know you love to dance, and that Sangria isn't just one of your favorite drinks." He leaned in kissing her on her cheek as he turned her softly, pulling her in ever so close with her back facing him. "You know how." Sam softly placed his finger over her lips to silence her. Sam had Pete teach him how to dance with the rhythm of the music, it seemed to fit this moment perfectly. Full of smooth and sensual moves, he never broke eye contact with Hanna. They moved with the wind, soft and sultry. The waitress peeking out the window to see honest love in the atmosphere.

"Come here, hurry," the waitress waved to the other workers. They stood there holding the curtains back just enough to take notice of Sam and Hanna with the romance that filled the night's sky. With every move, Hanna felt Sam's breath against her face. The rhythm, slow in motion, she could feel his strength next to her vulnerability. The smell of his rosewood and oak moss cologne overpowered her senses with an irresistible joy of living in the moment. He was close, in-tune with her wants and needs. Their steps although separate were one. Neither could feel the motions or movements of the dance but of floating. Beep, beep, beep, Hanna shook her head for an instant her headache had reappeared along with the chill to her bones. But she never broke eye contact with Sam, it was as if they were the only two people who existed in the world, it was a moment of awakening. Sam felt Hanna's love within his body as she did his.

11
CRASH

Hanna lay in her bed, somehow dreaming the most lucid of dreams. Sam walked into the room to take a second round of vitals as Pete sat up in his chair. "The doors wouldn't open, the train derailed, we were on our side. We were surrounded by metal walls, glass everywhere, water coming in from the creek and the cold from the blizzard was pouring onto us." Pete looked at Sam with such concern on his face. They had become the best of friends over the past two weeks while Hanna lay in a medically induced coma.

Sam finished his charting and sat down next to Pete. "Tell me everything, I know this is weighing heavily on you, but none of this was your fault."

"I promised to take care of our ladybug, I promised to keep her safe. I remember being thrown around like a rag doll, landing on my hands and knees. Amidst my own pain, all I was focused on was making my way to Hanna. I could see her fading into the murky waters, but I couldn't reach her. I was screaming agonizingly for her to answer me, Hanna! Hanna! Wake up beautiful, wake up my little ladybug!"

"Where did you get the name ladybug on such a short journey?"

Pete looked to Sam with sincere care in his eyes. "She's full of beauty and full of life under her anxiety and depression, with the right people surrounding her I saw she was able to let go of her worries and fears, I've also always heard that ladybugs bring a gift so to speak of renewal. Besides, they are stunning little creatures, look at her, she's a beauty."

"Pete, what else do you remember exactly? When Hanna comes out of this she is either going to remember everything or nothing. She suffered a severe concussion with an intracranial bleed, she will heal, trust me, but we had no choice but to place her in the state she is in for now. Pete, look at me, it was for her own good, she needs to heal."

Pete's eyes were exhausted and gloomy, "All I was trying to do was reach for her, screaming for her, saving her was worth more than saving myself." Tears fell from Pete's face, repeating bits and pieces of his story over and over. "I was one of the only passengers that was able to move. I remember seeing the sky turn colors of red and blue. Bright white lights shining down from the helicopters above. There seemed to be a thousand voices running towards us screaming if anyone could hear them, it's as if we were getting ready to explode. Axes, medical bags, face masks lined the broken windows looking in. Then I saw you and a few others climbing through them. I had her in my arms, I just kept yelling for help, I'm trained for disasters but had no supplies to be able to help her or anyone."

"Pete, you pulled her from the water, you kept her as warm as you could, you placed her scarf upon her head to help with the bleeding, even though unconscious, you were keeping her safe from further harm. I heard your call for help along with many others, but somehow, I was brought to you two."

Pete looked up at Sam, "The engineer came across after stating we were being redirected due to the storm, to telling passengers to brace themselves. But it was too late, the cars started rattling, the smell of terror and the metal from the grinding of the breaks burned my nose, our car filled with an awful stench and smoke, luggage was falling, cell phones and computers were being pelted like darts. People were being hurled into the air, including myself and Hanna. Seats were torn off the bolts, they became flying objects. Glass shattering, people screaming, bleeding. It was if a bomb had exploded and we were right in the middle of it. I know everything happened so fast, but it was as if our lives were being played in slow motion" Pete sat weeping, holding Hanna's hand.

Sam placed his hand on Pete's shoulder. "She will be fine, we just have to wait for the doctors to make a few more decisions on her care." They both sat quietly in conversation for a short while before Sam had to check on a couple of other patients.

Evening had turned to night, Pete laid quietly in the reclining chair taking his own medications for his broken rib and arm. He had managed to push his chair just close enough to Hanna to hold her hand while they slept. The rhythmic hissing of the ventilator somehow became soothing at night for Pete. He listened for the constant whoosh, pause, whoosh, pause. The now steady rhythm of her heart monitor echoed in the room and throughout the halls, proving that life was still inside of her. The days and nights were no longer plagued by fear. Pete could relax this night by the absence of noise, the abnormality of the tones from the machines. They had been taken over by the precise beeps of Hanna's heart and breaths.

As they lay in slumber Pete was awoken by an unnatural sound. "Oh Hanna, no!" He sprung from his chair hitting the emergency call button and screaming for help. Sam was charting a patient from the opposite end of the hall when he could hear Pete's scream, he ran to the hall to see that Hanna's red light was flashing over her door in room 430. Tunnel vision had set in as he ran towards her room yelling for the assistance of other staff. Entering Hanna's room Sam saw the panic in Pete's eyes, but he also saw that her respirator had been unplugged, the battery was running low. Sam calmed Pete quickly explaining that Hanna was ok. Pete's chair had somehow gotten entangled on the respirators cord causing it to come unplugged. Sam took a deep sigh of relief, ran a set of vitals on Hanna, adjusting the cords so that Pete could lay beside her.

"I get off at seven this morning, however, I'll be hanging around for a bit to see if the doctors have come up with a game plan. Please get some rest, she's safe. I'll sit in here for a bit until your comfortable again, I can work on my charting right here. Get some sleep, I won't go anywhere for now."

"I'll try, this whole thing has been overwhelming, worse than Nam." Pete tucked his pillow under his head and pulled his blanket back up around his neck, within just a few words he had fallen back into slumber.

Morning had come, Pete was still asleep holding onto Hanna. Sam had stayed over to listen in on what the doctors had in store for her care. He heard them speaking of slowing down the Propofol today allowing her to see if she will regain consciousness. With you here, it will help her to not awake overwhelmed. Weaning was their first option. Pete had started moving around after the doctors had left Hanna's room.

"Morning Pete," Pete looked over to see Sam sitting with Hanna's hand in his. The Doc was just in and they have put together a plan to wake our sleeping beauty. They plan on weaning her off the ventilator, taking her off slowly and hoping that she will start to breathe normally without difficulty. Pete looked at Sam with a puzzled look on his face. "What I mean is they will adjust her settings to allow her to attempt to breathe on her own, meaning Hanna will need to pick up most of the work while the ventilator will do less. She is showing so many signs of strength that they determined it's time."

"What if she isn't able to breathe?" Pete looked to Sam with concern. "Then they adjust the settings to take the work off Hanna, but you can't think like that, I've seen this plenty and if the doctors weren't sure she had it in her they would not be attempting it."

Hanna's parents could finally start their travel west to see to her. The storm's track had made it so difficult and at their age and own health issues, it didn't help matters. But with Pete and Sam giving them hourly updates, although sickened and afraid they knew their daughter was in the best possible care. It felt like forever since they had held their little girl, but their trip was drawing near and by the look of things they would make it there before she awoke. Pete had asked Sam to speak to her parents on the phone, just so that he would not miscommunicate what was going to be taking place. The phone call was short and sweet; however, Hanna's parents were only a couple of hours away and would soon be holding her hand.

Sam yawning, "Pete, if you don't mind I'm going to head down to my bunk room and try to get a few hours of sleep. Nothing will take place for about six hours, by then Hanna's parents will have spent some much-needed time with her and I can be here with you all when they start the process."

"Don't you have to work again tonight?" Pete looked up from Hanna's face.

"No, I'm off for the next two days so I can sleep later." Sam walked out of the room with a calm smile glancing back at Pete.

"Well it's just you and me ladybug, I wish I knew if you could actually hear me, what you've been dreaming about this whole time and if you are even going to remember me." Pete stood up and began pacing back and forth. "Hanna, you were my only concern along this journey, I'll never believe anything less than I was placed along with you on the same trip. That meeting Sam was in God's plans as well. Can you believe I'm hanging up my hat to go work for him, just wish you were going to be with us somehow? I feel like I've known you forever, forgive me for going through any belongings they found of yours, but I must say you are a survivor. Yes, I read through your journal, it's how I found out so much about you. I can only hope that your dreams come true." Hours passed as Pete consistently kept talking to Hanna.

Hanna's nurse walked into the room to let Pete know Hanna's parents had arrived and were asking for him. Pete gathered himself from all his emotions that he had been expressing while sitting and pacing quietly with Hanna. "Mr. and Mrs. Callaghan, hi I'm Pete." He extended his hand to both before Mrs. Callaghan grabbed him and hugged him tightly.

"You never left our little girl."

With tears welling in his eyes, "No ma'am, I knew she was my responsibility the first time I laid eyes on her and not for a moment did I intend on leaving her."

Mr. Callaghan extended his hand to Pete, "We could not have asked for better care of our little girl. Well, she's not so little anymore, but you understand."

"Yes sir, don't have any children of my own, but I would like to think if I had they would have been very similar to my little ladybug."

"Ladybug?" Hanna's mom spoke up. Letting out a bit of a laugh,

"Yes, I named her that on our journey. She's picture perfect, well-mannered and it just seems to fit." Pete turned to Hanna's door, "Are you ready to say hello to your little girl? She's been in great hands and they will be waking her here within the hour. I'm sure she is going to be very excited to see you."

They walked into the room very slowly. Her mom taking in all the wires and tubes that were connected to her daughter. She was focused on the heart monitor since that's the only one she knew. "Hanna, can you hear me? Its mama, dad is here too, look at you, you're sleeping so peaceful. We've been such a broken mess not being here and now that we are, I just want you to wake up."

Sam entered into Hanna's room, "Sam, this is Hanna's mom and dad, Mr. and Mrs. Callaghan.

"It's great to finally meet you," no hand extended, only arms wrapped around Hanna's mom and dad. We've been taking good care of your daughter. The doctors have been working around the clock to give her the best possible care, not to mention Pete. He has never left her side."

"Don't cut yourself so short Sam, he's been here as much as I have been on and off the clock."

"Did you know our Hanna before the accident?" "No sir, I was on the scene the night of the crash, she became my patient and with all the conversations that Pete and I have had, just could not leave her. She's made one hell of an impression on me, pardon my language." Sam walked over to the monitors to check on things and took a round of vitals just to pass a few moments of time.

"Hello everyone." Hanna's doctor had come into the room with his team to start the process of waking Hanna. "Sam, would you like to fill them in on what's going to take place and prepare them?"

"Yes sir, um why don't we all sit down for a moment. I've already explained to you on the phone what was going to take place but what you must remember is that Hanna may or may not remember who you are or even anything about the crash. It could be short term or long term, we're just not going to be sure until she comes out of this." He reached over and grabbed Mrs. Callaghan's hand. We're all in this together, she has a strong support system and once this part is over I still plan on being a part of Hanna's healing process."

Mrs. Callaghan looked up to him. "What do you mean?"

"She's going to need extended rehabilitation, we can talk about that later, but rather than a facility I think I have the perfect answer." Pete looked at Sam with a smile on his face. Without asking he already knew Sam's mind and what he was thinking. Sam had previously prepared a place for her in hopes of her parents agreeing.

The doctor kindly interrupted their conversation, "Are we ready to start the process? Sam why don't you grab a pair of gloves and help us out." Sam walked over to Hanna placing his gloves upon his hands. The doctor stopped the Propofol and administered another drug in case she was to awaken in an aggravated state. He then backed the vent down a couple of notches to see how she would respond. Sam turned to see Pete with his hands folded along with Mr. Callaghan's arms around Hanna's mom. After about ten minutes they watched the doctor turn the knob again to the left. Sam took a round of vitals, talking to Hanna in a calming voice.

"You have a room full of people that love you waiting to say hello Hanna. You're doing great, you can do this, keep fighting beautiful." Pete looked to Sam with the heaviness fading from his heart. What felt like an eternity had come to an end quickly. Well, everyone, she is breathing on her own." The doctor stepped in at that moment and unsecured the tube and deflated the cuff. Removing the tube, he gently pulled it from Hanna's mouth.

Doc turned to Sam, "Sam I need you to stay with our patient until I return."

"Yes sir, I'm not going anywhere."

"Fine, keep me updated, I'll have a nurse come in and keep a check on her vitals every twenty minutes. I'm going to put the orders in place for a few more scans to double check everything on Hanna. If she begins to wake you know what to do but call for me immediately."

"Yes, sir."

It had been about three hours, Hanna was holding her own, breathing normally and vital signs all looking positive. Sam and Pete were in conversation sitting next to Hanna with her parents on the other side of her. Sam looked down, with a shocked smile on his face, "She squeezed my hand. Hanna are you with us beautiful?" He immediately hit the call button for the nurse and upon her entry, he instructed her to contact the doctor immediately. Doc Bradley was charting at the nurse's station when the nurse's bell from Hanna's room started to ring.

"Doc, she squeezed my hand, any moment she should be waking up." Pete and Sam moved out of the way so that Doc Bradley could examine her. Upon looking at her pupils Hanna blinked. "Are you with us Hanna?' Hanna blinked again as if coming out of a normal groggy slumber. "Hanna, if you can hear me can you squeeze my hand?' He asked the question in fifteen-second intervals, Hanna responding after a couple of minutes. She tried to speak but everyone could tell she was fighting to speak. Doc Bradley reassured everyone that this was normal. After such a lengthy time on the ventilator her throat was raw, however, they had medications to help with that as well. The most significant thing right now was that she was waking up and everything seemed to be going in the positive direction that all had been praying for. Hanna's dad had gone down to the cafeteria to get her mother something to drink. Sam sat beside Hanna holding her hand still talking to her in a soft voice.

Pete and Hanna's mom were caught up in conversation about the happenings that unfolded the night of the crash. "I dreamt of you." Hanna had vocalized four words, Sam looked up to see those beautiful green eyes that Pete had spoken of.

"Hanna are you with us beautiful?"

"I dreamt of you."

"Dreamt of who Hanna?" Sam was not worried but concerned about her words.

"You, Sam, I dreamt of you. Where's Pete?" Pete's ears perked up, hearing his name coming from the angelic voice was worth more than anything on earth to him at this moment.

"Your mom and dad are here also Hanna." Hanna's mom and Pete made their way over by her bed. Her mom leaned over to hug her with tears of joy in her eyes.

"We thought we had lost you, baby. You had us so worried."

"I called you and told you I was safe with Pete and Sam."

Her mom looked over to Sam, "What's wrong?"

"Hanna, do you know where you are?" Sam had grasped her hand with both of his at this moment.

"Well I think I'm in the hospital by the looks of things, did I have a concussion from falling down the stairs at the carriage house?" Hanna turned her attention to her mom, "I had an attack mom and fell down the stairs, I'm all right though, right?"

Pete looked over to Hanna, "Ladybug, we were in a train crash, do you remember any of it?"

"No, we weren't silly, we've been staying with Sam at the Inn," She looked over to Sam and squeezed his hand, "Is Cloe ok? I miss her." Hanna had the most genuine look on her face speaking to Sam.

"How, never mind, yes, Cloe is great, and she misses you also." Hanna faded back off to sleep which was expected, however, Sam and Pete were very confused. How did she know about the Inn or even Cloe? Answers would come but for now, they were left only with Hanna and the unknown.

12
SECOND CHANCES

Sam and Pete were caught up in conversation, catching Hanna's mom and dad up on the day to day happenings that had occurred since the night of the crash. By no means had Hanna ever visited the Inn, much less met Cloe. Hanna's mom enlightened them a bit about their daughter. "Hanna is a special person, she has always had a special gift, but mostly feeling the emotions of the living and departed. With that comes the good and the bad. She loves the woods and water, she is centered there, at peace. Hanna has always dreamt of the perfect love, the kind that is intoxicating. The one that is overwhelming to your senses yet knowing that the two have enough energy and fight in them to keep the relationship fresh. She has other qualities that she has had since a little girl, but those aren't for me to discuss, that would be for Hanna to tell you."

"I'm just stumped over her knowing about the carriage house, the Inn, Cloe." Pete turned to Sam, "Do you think she could actually hear our conversations that took place around her?"

Sam rubbing his head, "There has been evidence of coma patients hearing certain voices around them, and feeling people who touch them, anything is possible. I just can't wait for her to wake fully enough to hear her story."

Sam and Pete took Hanna's parents outside of the room and sat them down. "The doctors will be coming in to take Hanna for scans in a bit. Just to make sure swelling and anything else has subsided enough for her to be discharged in a couple of days, however, she is going to need some long-term care. Have you thought about what you would like to do?"

Hanna's mom looked at her father, "Can't we take her home with us?"

"No, that won't be an option right now, she will need to be close to the facility just in case for a while. There is a rehabilitation facility down the street, however, I think I have a better plan."

Hanna's father spoke up, "We're listening," as he sat back in the chair with his arms folded.

"Well, I've been thinking. After the crash Pete and I became friends very quickly, I own a bed and breakfast about a mile and a half away from here. Long story, I kept it going for my parents after they passed away. Pete is going to be working for me along with a couple who were very good friends of my parents for years. They all but lost their home during the storm." Sam took a moment to gather his words, "I think Hanna should stay at the Inn. I only work three shifts here a week, the rest of the time I am at the Inn where I reside in the guest house. I only finished it a few days ago, for it had been used mostly for storage. However, after talking to Pete so much I started thinking about Hanna and thought it would be the perfect place for her to completely heal."

Hanna's mom spoke up, "All right, and if we were to do this who will take care of her the days you are working, and do you even have enough time to run your family business with her there?"

"Well, I figured for the first couple of weeks I would keep her in one of the rooms at the Inn, that way everyone is around at all times, you, of course, could stay in the lower level bedroom for as long as you like or come and go as your able to, I never rent that one out. I can promise you she would be well taken care of, but I honestly just think Hanna having more one on one and feeling at home instead of being a number in a facility would be better for her physical and emotional health."

"But your busy season is coming, we can't take money away from you," Hanna's mom broke into tears.

"It would not, not at all. Pete has taken two rooms on the top floor that will be turned into an apartment, Mr. and Mrs. Whittle have taken the other two rooms on the top floor and will be doing the same, they are equipped with living and bedroom spaces along with bathrooms. I have an extra room upstairs that has a balcony overlooking the property with its own private bath, it has a large gathering area as soon as you get off the elevator, so she could feel free to sit and watch tv or just stay in her room and because of the elevator we could get her out and about so to speak after a couple of weeks to allow her full run of the Inn."

"But how would you and Pete or the Whittles hear her if she needed anything or God forbid start to go backwards."

"Well with your approval I would sleep upstairs in her room, I have a foldable cot that I can place in her room. Pete would be right upstairs in shouting distance and you all on the lower level in the spare room. When I'm working everyone would just take shifts sitting with her until I got home. I even thought about purchasing a unit to place in her room so that if she needed anything we would be able to hear her. It won't be easy, but it's so much better than a facility."

Pete walked over to Hanna's bed grasping her hand, "We just adore her and would do anything for her. Mr. and Mrs. Callaghan, she has touched my life; Sam's life more than you could ever know. It's like she belongs here. We all three were meant to be together the night of the crash, she was meant to have a second chance."

Doc Bradley entered Hanna's room, "I'm going to have the orderly take Hanna down for a few scans now. I just want to be sure she is heading in the right direction after taking her off the ventilator. Her pressure and pulse look good, she's been awake off and on, but with Sam's message of not knowing what she was speaking of earlier we just want to be sure." The orderly gathered her vital pack placing it on her gurney along with her fluids, carefully lowered her head down, unlocked the wheels and began to roll her out of the room.

"Sam, Sam," her voice was in sheer panic.

"I'm right here Hanna, what's wrong? Are you hurting?"

"No, where am I going, I don't want to be by myself." Tears were rolling down her face, trying to speak with an irritation in her throat. Sam quieted her down quickly holding her hand and talking to her as they headed down the hall.

"You see," Pete looked at Mr. and Mrs. Callaghan, "She's never met Sam until a couple of hours ago, but it seems like they have had a life together in the past." Hanna watched the lights flutter by above her, one after one. Sam had not stopped speaking to her, he spoke of the Inn and taking her there with her parents to allow her the time she needed.

He began to describe the grounds when Hanna looked over to him. "Can I have the Lilac room back? I love that room, it's so comfortable and cozy. Watching the snow fall from the chair at night brings peace to me." Sam gazed into Hanna's eyes and assured her that he would see what he could do. Not a word was spoken of how she knew the name of the room or that the old winged back chair faced the trees and the snow. Hanna gave him a huge smile before falling back to sleep.

Sam was stumped at the remarks that Hanna had been making, however, what she didn't know was that Sam was holding a secret of his own. The imaging was complete, and Hanna was headed back to room 430. She was still in slumber, Sam still holding her hand as if out of habit. The waiting game had begun, minute after minute, hour after hour. From pacing, back and forth to sitting in chairs, not many words were expressed, silence seemed to take over. "Sam," Hanna had woken startled by her surroundings. "I hear the beeping again."

"What beeping Hanna?" Sam while still holding on to her hand was confused yet intrigued.

"I have been hearing beeping for a while now. I heard it the night we had to stop in your beautiful town, I heard it in the Lilac room, the carriage house, the gathering room, on our date and I'm hearing it now." She looked up, "That machine is making the same sounds that have been playing over and over in my head."

"Hanna, that's your heart monitor beautiful, you've been in the hospital for a couple of weeks now. The train you were on crashed, you have been here in a coma and we've all been waiting for you to heal enough and wake up."

"No, no, you're wrong, it's all wrong." Her anxiety was taking over her body. In a confused state of mind, Hanna tried reminding Pete that she had been at the Inn with him the entire time. "I'm here because I fell down the stairs and hit my head, that's why it hurts."

"Ok, right now I need you to calm down and just breathe for me. Your right, you did hit your head, but you're getting better now and within a few weeks you'll be as good as new." Sam stroked Hanna's head, "Just breathe."

"You told me that on our first date." Hanna quickly drifted back off to sleep holding tightly onto Sam's hand. Sam just sat there beside her brushing her hair away from her face.

Mrs. Callaghan spoke up, "Sam, are you sure you and Hanna have never met?"

"Yes ma'am, I just happened to be the nurse on the scene that night, she has been my patient on rotation ever since."

Hanna's mom was confused, "I've never seen her smile the way she does with you, it's as if she's known you forever. Heck, I don't even think she realizes any of us are here right now."

"Well she's going to know, I need to step out for a bit, Pete can you take my place and Mr. and Mrs. Callaghan, why don't you sit on her left. She seems to be waking every fifteen minutes or so. I just want to go check on the scans, see if the doctors have heard anything yet." He let go of Hanna's hand slowly, placing her hand into Pete's. Pete watched Sam walk out of the room with his head down, he watched Sam's hands cradle his face wiping what seemed to be tears from his face. As fast as he fell apart he pulled himself back together as he walked out of sight.

Pete excused himself from the room as well making an excuse of visiting the cafeteria for something to drink. Walking down the halls he stopped a couple of nurses to figure out where Sam had gone. He found him in a closed room with at least ten images up on a wall. Sam was smiling with excitement as tears rolled down his face. He watched the Doc and Sam exchange a quick hug before Sam departed from the room.

"Pete, are you lost?"

"No sir, just came to check on you, make sure you were all right."

"I'm more than all right, Hanna can come home in a couple of days, but there is so much to get ready for her and her parents and honestly I don't want to leave her."

"Home, you mean the Inn?" "Yeah, yes, that's what I meant."

"Well her mom and dad are here, I would be more than happy to go with you to tidy up whatever rooms you're going to use. It will be nice to escape here for a couple of hours, besides not having our ladybug with us." Sam walked down to the cafeteria with Pete to purchase some drinks and a couple of lunches for Hanna's mom and dad. Strolling back to the room they found Hanna awake again and although not talking much she knew who her mom and dad were, she smiled as Pete walked in and held out her arms for him.

Pete walked over, "Well hello my little ladybug, it sure is nice to see those beautiful green eyes again."

"Oh Pete, you act like it's been forever, her hug was filled with warmth but weak. Mom and dad, this man right here took such good care of me, he reminds me of Uncle Patrick, always there picking up the pieces so that I didn't fall apart. Hanna's smile filled the room, the warmth of her soul reached inside of Sam's heart.

"Well, little ladybug, the doctors are going to be in soon to talk to you and your parents. Sam and I are going to go over to the Inn for a couple of hours to get your room ready along with a room for your mom and dad. You know just straighten up."

"You'll be back, right?" Hanna had a bit of anxiety sweeping over her.

"Of course," Sam's head peeking into the room. A couple of hours tops, is there anything you want us to bring you?"

"My blanket from my carry-on bag would be nice. I hate not having it here with me." Sam gave half a smile, nodding his head.

"I'll do my best, be back soon Hanna." Pete gently got up grabbing what was left of her bag from under her bed and headed out the door quickly for her not to notice it.

Sam and Pete had made their way back to the Inn by the back roads due to the heavy snow that consumed most of the highway. "Mrs. Whittle, what are you up to?"

"Oh, nothing dear, just baking a ton of cookies for the upcoming guests next week." She smiled, as she continued to use her favorite snowflake cookie cutter.

"Well, we are making room for three more guests."

"Three more?" She asked with a concerned look in her eyes.

"Yes, Hanna, one of my patients at the hospital needs a place to recuperate over the next four to six weeks, her mom and dad will be here till Thanksgiving with us and then back again the week of Christmas."

"Recuperate? Is this the girl you spoke of from the train accident?"

"Yes, ma'am, she is beautiful, her smile just warms a room, but there is something mysterious about her that is so intriguing that she leaves me wanting to know more about her." Sam and Pete headed back towards Sam's old room with Mrs. Whittle following.

"Mrs. Whittle, I know we have someone booked for the Lilac room, did they actually ask for that room specifically?"

"Well no dear, just wanted a reservation."

"Thank God, ok the game plan is to put Hanna's parents in mom and dad's old room and place our guests here in my old room, lower level, easier for them to enjoy the first floor and the fireplaces. Hanna will be in the Lilac room, I'll be putting a cot in the room for myself, just so that I can keep an eye on her. Pete will be watching over her on the days that I'm working and if you wouldn't mind taking her up lunch and a snack at night I would be ever so grateful, oh and one more thing." Mrs. Whittle and Pete looked at Sam inquisitive to what was next. "I'm bringing Cloe over from the guest house to keep Hanna company. I figured yours and Mr. Whittle's suite is together enough to live in along with Pete's, so we aren't in need of any other rooms, we will have one available and that will be my old room if we need it."

"Nice game plan there slick," Pete letting out a slight laugh.

"What does that mean?" Sam looked over to Pete.

"It means you are falling for this girl who you don't even know yet, it means your heart is so full of joy and peace that we haven't seen in a long time."

Mrs. Whittle strolled into Sam's old room with clean sheets that she laid upon the queen size antique bed. "Well maybe, Pete kept her alive, he saved her, they have a connection that only those two will ever understand. For me, yes, I want to get to know her, what better way than to have her recover right here with all of us." Pete and Mrs. Whittle glanced at each other with a smile upon their faces.

Pete and Sam worked vigorously on completing the room for their guests, boxes being moved to the shed, mopping and cleaning of the floors along with a large 7-foot pine and two extra boxes from the attic that held Christmas decorations to enhance the room. For Mrs. Whittle, she was making sure that everything was just perfect in Sam's parent's old room for the arrival of Hanna's parents. Knowing that they were going to fill the house with so much love for the holidays seemed to give Mrs. Whittle the twinkle back in her eyes that had been missing for quite some time. The Callaghan's and Hanna were the missing pieces of the puzzle.

13
ENLIGHTEN ME

Hanna's parents were speaking to the doctors when Sam and Pete arrived back to the hospital. "Doc Bradley is everything all right?" Sam seemed concerned to see him in Hanna's room.

"Everything is great, Hanna why don't you fill them in on the good news?" Doc Bradley gave her a wink and patted Sam on the shoulder as he exited the room.

With suspense in his voice, "So?" Hanna's smile was electrifying.

Mrs. Callaghan walked over to Pete giving him a huge hug. "You made all of this possible you know." She laid her hands upon both sides of Pete's face staring directly into his eyes.

"I get to leave tomorrow! They are getting me a wheelchair, walker, oh and look!" Sam and Pete looked at the blanket that Hanna was holding in her hand.

"Where did you get that?" Pete looking at Hanna puzzled, knowing it was never found in her carry on that he had taken back to the Inn.

"Funny, a nurse brought it into me, she said that numerous items had been found at the crash and she knew it was mine because my grandmother had stitched my name on the inside corner. I told her it must have just gotten laid down somewhere that I wasn't in any crash." Hanna smelled her blanket as she asked her mom to cover her with it. Sam walked out of the room to catch the Doc before he left the nurses station.

"Doc, Hanna isn't remembering anything from the crash but still is showing signs of the anxiety that Pete spoke of. He stated she had a pill bottle in her hand for anti-anxiety and panic attacks. Is there any way we can find out what she was on and have it on hand in case she needs it, or God forbid when she starts remembering what happened?"

The Doc looked at Sam with sincerity in his face, "Let me speak to her parents, see if we can figure out who her provider was and get her medical records, I'm more than happy to get her on something to help with the transition, the poor thing will end up in therapy if she starts to remember and isn't prepared." The Doc walked off to his next round of patients.

Sam entered Hanna's room once again to find his sleeping beauty fast in slumber. Her special blanket tucked around her as to keep her safe. With her mom and dad beside her watching her sleep. "Mr. and Mrs. Callaghan, do you happen to know who Hanna's doctors were in her hometown? We are trying to figure out which medications she was on for her anxiety and panic attacks."

"No, she kept her private life private." Mrs. Callaghan leaned over to hold Hanna's hand, watching her sleep. "Although, when she came to visit I remember two medications that she was taking. I only know because one night she had an attack and I had to go into her purse and wasn't sure which one she needed, so I took her both. One began with a Z and the other, the one she needed was Xanax."

"All right, that's a great start, if she's taking Xanax than most likely the Z word is Zoloft, it's used to help with anxiety, panic attacks and post-traumatic disorder along with other disorders. You are sure about this right?" Sam turned back to Hanna's parents.

Pete spoke up, "Sam, Xanax is it, that's the medication she was holding on the train, I have no idea of the dosage, but that's the one." Sam nodded his head, as he once again left the room to find Doc. Everything was going as planned, Hanna could leave the hospital tomorrow, her mom and dad able to shower and sleep in peace. Sam had the doctor to sign off on two prescriptions along with what she would need to finish healing. Now it was nothing more than a wait and see game of when Hanna would remember. Sam prayed he would be at the Inn with Pete when it happened, for he knew it was going to be a struggle, Hanna was going to need all the support she could get surrounding her.

The day had come, Hanna was being released. Papers were being signed, the nurse was able to find clothes to fit her for her ride to the Inn. Her original clothes had been cut off in the back of the ambulance and for what was left in her carry on, it was mostly personal belongings with only one change of clothes and a nightgown. Hanna's father went to fetch their car, bringing it around to the front of the hospital where he would meet up with Pete. Hanna would ride with her mom and dad, Sam in the back with Hanna, following behind Pete. The nurse strolled Hanna down to the front doors where Sam helped Hanna into the back seat of her dad's car. "Ok, we are only about five minutes away, go slow on the backroads they haven't been plowed very well yet, pull up under the carport when we arrive. It will be easier to get Hanna into the Inn that way." Hanna's dad nodded as he made his way onto the snow-covered roads.

It was still very cold, with the nightly wind chill getting to below zero. Mounds of what was fluffy and glistening snow lined the streets covered in mud and dirt. "Mom, I can't wait for you to see the Inn, Sam has done so much work to it, it's the most amazing place I've ever seen, and Sam" Hanna glancing into his eyes. "We still need to decorate the Lilac and Magnolia rooms for Christmas."

Sam just looked at Hanna in disbelief of how she knew any of this. Pete arrived just before Mr. Callaghan. He had Hanna's wheelchair set up on the porch with Mrs. Whittle waiting at the door with an extra blanket freshly warmed from the dryer.
Sam carried Hanna up on to the porch placing her into the wheelchair. Pete pardoned himself to help Mr.

Callaghan gather their luggage while helping Mrs. Callaghan across the parking lot and up the stairs.

"Hello dear, welcome." Hanna was wheeled into the house greeted by Mrs. Whittle.

"Hi Mrs. Whittle, so happy to see you again, it feels like I've been gone forever." Sam quickly shot Mrs. Whittle a glance, nodding his head as in to not ask any questions. Through the doors with a nice comfy warm blanket laid upon Hanna's lap, Sam whispered to Mrs. Whittle that he would explain later and for now to just go with it. Pete showed Hanna's parents to their room.

"Why don't you guys get comfortable and meet us in the dining room in about an hour. Mr. Whittle has made a dinner fit for a king I do believe by the smell of things." He let out a little laugh while turning on the fireplace in their new home for the meantime. Sam pushed Hanna into the gathering room and sat down beside her on the couch. "Do you want to go upstairs and lay down until dinner? You must be exhausted."

Hanna leaned over to Sam, "Can I tell you a secret? I am so happy to not be laying in a bed, I just want to sit here with you and enjoy the glow of the fireplace." Sam sat quietly for a few moments before getting up to grab his medical bag.

"I promised Doc I would keep an eye on your vitals over the next couple of days, is your head hurting at all?"

"Nope, but I told you something was wrong from the fall. I just didn't realize I had been in the hospital for almost two weeks. And Mrs. Whittle, why did she look at me so oddly when we came in the door?"

"Well, I think Mrs. Whittle has overdone herself the past couple of days. When Pete and I got here yesterday she was baking up a storm getting ready for our guests this week." He glanced at Hanna while taking her blood pressure giving off a grin. "Hey Pete," Sam gave him that look as to just go with things, can you sit here with Hanna while I go help Mrs. Whittle get the table set?"

"Absolutely, it will give me and ladybug here some time to sit and relax."

Sam walked down the hall into the kitchen to give the Whittles a hand with dinner. He gathered the dishes and silverware whistling as he went into the dining room. He came back for the glasses and a couple of bottles of wine. He put the coffee on along with a pot of hot tea. "Oh Sam, I made my caramel hot chocolate as well, I placed it in the kettle on the stove to keep it warm." Sam walked slowly to the dining room where he set up all the drinks on the buffet, he took the coffee cups from underneath and laid them out as well. Mr. and Mrs. Callaghan came into the kitchen making small talk to the Whittles while helping to gather dinner to take into the dining room, placing it gently upon the table. Hanna's mom peeked into the gathering room.

"Hey guys, dinner is ready." Pete turned to see a smile upon Hanna's mom's face. "Your mom seems to be settling in just fine here, first time I've seen a smile on her face since meeting her."

Hanna looked up at Pete, "Why wouldn't she? This place is magical, it brings out the best in people." Pete stood from the couch pushing Hanna into the dining room.

"Mr. Whittle went all out, he's been trying some of his recipes that he hasn't made in quite some time." They all sat around the table with the smell of freshly baked bread and garlic shrimp pasta. The salad was exquisite alone with his homemade vinaigrette dressing.

Before passing their plates around Hanna spoke up. "Can we say grace tonight?" Everyone looked towards Hanna for a brief quiet moment.

Mrs. Whittle's eyes lit up, "Of course, now everyone gather hands." For the first time Sam and Hanna connected, Sam had always been the one holding Hanna's hand with no response in return, however, this night, the grip of complete love and content was exchanged between the two. Pete chimed in to say a prayer before engaging in dinner. It was sweet and to the point, however near the end, he mentioned the unwelcomed circumstances that turned strangers into family. Hanna's mom shed a tear, her dad although delighted about the meal they were about to eat, cleared his throat rubbing his eyes.

"What is everyone so gloomy for? Mom, dad, I told you this place was magnificent, I honestly can't wait to get started on the job, well as soon as I'm healed." Nudging Sam in his arm with a bright smile. Dinner conversation stayed light and turned away from the storm, it was focused more on decorating the Lilac room and putting the finishing touches on the Magnolia suite. Mrs. Whittle spoke of all the fine desserts she had in store along with Mr. Whittle's recipes of the past. Pete had stood to refill his cup of coffee, Hanna's mom and dad shared a glass of wine along with the Whittles, Sam stuck to water along with Hanna in hopes that she would ask no questions. During laughter and reminiscing of Hanna as a child, Mrs. Whittle excused herself to fetch the Pecan pie she had baked earlier in the day.

"All right everyone, last part of the meal. Hot tea, coffee, and my homemade caramel coffee hot chocolate are on the buffet along with whipped cream for the pie.

"Mom, Hanna spoke up with excitement, you have to try Mrs. Whittle's hot chocolate. She puts real caramel in it as well, I swear it fills your mouth with joy." Mrs. Whittle looked over at Hanna, Sam glancing over to Mrs. Whittle with a nod, closing his eyes.

"I don't understand why on earth everyone hushes up and acts as if someone has died every time I speak of the Inn or the food or..."

Hanna was cut off by Sam's quick thinking. "Hanna you're looking pretty exhausted. I promised Doc that if he allowed you to leave the hospital that I would have you resting, so far today, we haven't gotten you to rest for one second." He shot Hanna a quick smile, "what do you say we take our dessert upstairs? Your mom can help get you changed and if you're in the mood for a shower I have a shower seat all set up for you. Everyone else can go enjoy the fireplace in the gathering room while I clean up."

"Nonsense, there's too much to do," Mr. Whittle spoke up.

"Mr. Whittle you and the Mrs. have done more than your fair share around here the past week with me being at the hospital so much. I just want you all to relax tonight, take the day off tomorrow, no work, just relax. I'm forever grateful for everything you've been doing, I really am. I'm not sure what I did without you from the beginning." Sam smiled as he excused himself from the table. Pete helped Hanna's mom to the elevator with Hanna in hand, strolling her into her room for the night, leaving them to have some mother, daughter time. As he closed the door he let out a sigh of relief, whistling as he marched down the stairs turning the corner into the kitchen.

"Want some help?" Pete immediately pitched in drying dishes and putting them away while Sam washed. Mr. and Mrs. Whittle along with Hanna's dad had taken Sam's advice enjoying dessert in front of the fire in the gathering room for a relaxing conversation.

"Pete, when are we going to talk to Hanna? I think sooner rather than later, maybe even tonight once she gets herself comfortable."

Pete had a concerned look on his face, "Too soon, ya think?"

"No, not really, I think the sooner she comes to grips with what happened it's less likely to sneak up on her when we might not be around."

"Point taken, we can talk to her tonight once she's in bed." Hanna's mom yelled down the stairs that she needed help with Hanna.

Sam looked at Pete and took off up the stairs. "What's wrong? Is Hanna ok?"

"Yes, she wanted to take a shower and I can't get her back up, she's still not able to stand long enough for me to get her dried off."

"All right, that's an easy fix." Sam grabbed the robe off the bathroom door and had her mom throw it around Hanna.

"Hanna, can you put your arms through for me?"

"Sure, sorry, I just got a little loopy there for a minute."

"It's ok, the medications will do that to you not to mention you haven't rested at all today." Before her mom knew it, while he was lost in conversation with Hanna he had managed to get the robe around her, a towel upon her head and had picked her up and laid her upon the bed, drying off all parts that were considered safe zones. "Mom, where is Hanna's nightgown and undergarments?"

"Um, they're right here." "Ok, I'm turning around while mom gets your lower half dressed, next I'll sit you up from behind so that we can get the robe off you and finish drying you off, mom can slip your nightgown on from there. Before they knew it, Hanna was dressed. Mrs. Callaghan brushing out her hair, placing a dry towel upon her pillow for her beautiful dampened hair. Hanna was comfortable under the blankets propped up with feather down pillows to enjoy the whisper of the fireplace. Hanna's mom was exhausted, yawning as she spoke to her daughter.

"Mrs. Callaghan, you're so tired, I've got everything we need up here for the night including some hot chocolate that I fetched from the kitchen. Hanna are you ok up here while I take your mom downstairs?"

"Yes, letting out a yawn herself, I'm fine, mom you and dad get some rest. Maybe tomorrow we can decorate this room for Christmas." Hanna closed her eyes with a subtle smile upon her face. Sam walked with Hanna's mom down the stairs and into the gathering room with everyone else. I'm going to head back upstairs with Hanna and monitor her tonight. Before I go, does anyone need anything?"

All heads bowed, "Is everything ok?" Sam felt a chill in the room.

Mr. Callaghan spoke up, "Just wondering when Hanna will end up remembering all of this? It's taken a toll on the four of us in this room, I can't imagine what it's going to do to Hanna when she realizes nothing has been real that she has spoken of since waking up." Hanna's dad wrapped his arms around Mrs. Callaghan. "Sam, Pete, remember I told you that Hanna needed to tell you for herself what she experiences?" They both shook their heads. "Well Hanna is gifted, she feels and sees things that we could never imagine. From picking up on other emotions to feeling the unliving and sometimes how they passed. Don't treat her like a virus or as if she's crazy, this has been going on since she was a little girl. It went silent for a very long time, with each passing death in the family along with sickness it kicked back up. I think she truly believes she lives here with you all. There's no surprise really that she knows so much about this place, she's been guided if that makes any sense?"

Pete broke the silence, "So, Hanna is gifted?"
"Yes, but not scary gifted, she's what they call an empath. However, somehow she is blocking out everything that has happened to her."

Sam spoke up, "Or has she?" If she has been dealing with a lot lately, off her medications since the accident, hearing us all speak of the Inn and what is happening around it, everything could have unfolded in her dreams, keeping her safe even though she knows the truth. It's her comfort zone, she knows everyone around here will help her heal. She said it herself, this place is magical," he looked up to the Whittles. "She's right. There are spirits here, good ones, mom use to call them the Guardians of the Inn. Past customers have spoken of them. This place is indeed magical."

Sam turned towards the hallway, Pete speaking up, "Hanna will be good for this place, the spark in her eyes says it all. She needs to feel wanted, needed, without that I think that's when her anxiety and panic attacks kick in, but who am I, just an old marine." Everyone sat in silence for a moment before saying their goodnights as they went off to slumber. Pete and Sam walked up the stairs and into Hanna's room.

A quiet knock on the door, "Hanna are you awake?"

Her angelic voice echoed in the room with excitement, "Come in, come in." Sam opened the door as he and Pete entered. Pete was carrying some of Mrs. Whittle's hot chocolate and a small plate of cookies for Hanna. "Oh my, this my favorite part of the night."

"Yes ma'am, only the best for my ladybug."

Hanna smiled with excitement, "I tell ya, this beats a hospital bed any day of the week. I love soft beds and these pillows! I didn't know how much I missed them." Sam sat down on the bed next to Hanna while Pete walked over sitting in the winged backed chair.

"Hanna, do you remember anything from the crash, anything at all?"

She looked to Sam and glanced over to Pete, "Why do you all keep speaking of a crash? Do you not want me here anymore Sam?"

"No, no, it's not that, I'm just confused on how you know so much of the Inn and all of us here as if you have lived here your whole life when up until today, it was your first time here."

"No, Pete and I came here two weeks ago, we fell in love, you got Cloe for me, Cloe? Where's Cloe? I fell coming down the stairs in the guest house that you fixed up for us, don't you remember?" Pete left the room to go fetch Cloe from the Whittles before they fell asleep for the night. When he returned

Hanna was in tears, Sam's arms wrapped tightly around her. "I remember the train ride, meeting Pete who was such a breath of fresh air, he was my missing link on the trip." Sam listened as she went on. "The conductor told us to brace that there was a major storm and that we would be stuck here in Hunter's Grove for a few days. Pete made all the arrangements for us to stay here with you, life took over and we became a part of the Inn along with you and the Whittles."

"Hanna, baby, you and Pete were in a train accident, you have been my patient since it happened. Haven't you been curious as to why Pete's arm is in a sling and he's wearing a girdle around his chest?"

"Cloe come here baby girl." Pete handed Cloe over to Hanna with a smile. Cloe seemed content with someone she had never met. She curled up in her arms and drifted off to sleep. Hanna turned to Pete, "Is what Sam's saying the truth? Were we in a train accident?"

Pete got up and walked over to the bed sitting on the side. "Yes ladybug, we were in a crash, I thought I had lost you."

"So, I don't live here, I don't have a job here," she looked at Sam, "We aren't in love and I still live in, in, oh my God, where do I live?" Hanna fell apart.

"You live here Hanna, for now, or until we figure things out or if you decide to stay, you live here." Sam wrapped his arms around Hanna. He could not understand how he had feelings for a person who he was only able to talk to for the first time a couple of days before. He listened to Pete's stories, listened to how much love was within Hanna's soul, she was beautiful even in a coma.

Pete excused himself for the night. "Good night my ladybug," kissing Hanna upon the forehead, "I told you on the train I would take care of you, I don't go back on my word, I'll see you in the morning beautiful."

"Pete," Hanna managed to get out a word from her tears, she wrapped her arms around him, "Thank you." Pete's arms embraced Hanna as well before he slightly pulled away giving her that half smile, nodding his head as if he had a cowboy hat on, "Sweet dreams princess."

Sam continued to lay in bed with Hanna, talking about how he became the owner of the Inn, he held Hanna in his arms and Cloe was now content laying at the foot of the bed. "Lord I almost forgot, I need to take your vitals and record them tonight along with giving you your medications. Do you still have something to drink?"

"Yes, enough to swallow a couple of pills." Sam handed her the medications as he wrote down her numbers on the paper.

"All looks good besides being a little upset and anxious tonight. I'll let you get comfortable, but I'll be right here on the cot beside you."

"Sam, can you sleep up here? I'm not sure what is going on if I have amnesia, if I'm going insane, but I know for tonight I would like you to sleep beside me."

"Absolutely, and by the way, you're not insane, you're dealing with a traumatic incident, it's ok to feel everything you're feeling." He situated his pillows, propped up slightly above Hanna. Took her into his arms and held her tightly until she fell asleep.

Christmas in Hunter's Grove

14
DON'T LET ME FALL

Morning had come, Hanna was sitting in the winged back chair staring out the window at the snow-covered trees. She seemed to be in a daze as she was quiet with her grandmother's blanket covering her. "Good morning Hanna are you, all right?" Hanna turned her head towards Sam acknowledging his presence.

"Yes, just sitting here trying to make sense of everything." She turned gazing back out the window. Sam got out of bed and turned the fireplace up a bit, with a chill in the air he didn't want Hanna catching a cold.

"Hanna, do you remember anything?"

Gazing out the window, "I had a cold, you all nursed me back to health, I remember running a fever, being cold, so cold. But you took care of me. I remember falling down the stairs from a panic attack and having the worst headache. Pete and I showed up at your Inn the night of the storm. I remember seeing blue, green and red lights streamed across the streets. Decorating the Inn, moving Mr. and Mrs. Whittle into their new space upstairs along with Pete. Picking up Cloe from Janice and the beautifully decorated carriage house that you made for us. I remember everything, but you and Pete keep saying I was in a crash. Oh wait, I even remember my little ghost boy."

"Ghost boy?"

"Yes, he blew me raspberries one morning, he's made faces at me and likes to lay in bed with me and just stare into my eyes." Sam sat there so concerned, Hanna had described so many situations that had taken place at the Inn, without her being there with them. She was so sure of herself, he sat there lost in conversation for over an hour while Hanna spoke of everything they had done together. Hanna's way of speaking when she was excited was in her hand gestures, everything sent chills up Sam's spine.

A knock came to the door. Sam quietly turned the knob opening it slowly. "Good morning everyone, how are you doing Hanna?" Hanna's mom was dressed and in what appeared to be a great mood. "I helped Mrs. Whittle make breakfast, nothing fancy. We've got pancakes, sausage, bacon and eggs, hope that's fine with everyone? Mrs. Whittle even has fresh orange juice, coffee and her famous hot chocolate ready."

"Mom I'm still in my nightgown."

Hanna's mother turned to Sam, "He is still in his pajamas, but you don't hear him complaining, come on, you need to eat while it's hot, there's time for a shower and to get dressed after breakfast." Sam smiled, laughing under his breath. Hanna's mom reminded him of his late mother in a way. No nonsense and right to the point. Hanna walked to the wheelchair with her blanket laying across her lap.

"Well you heard my mom, let's go." Sam laughed as he made his way down the hall pushing Hanna towards the elevator.

"Breakfast won't take long, then you can get yourself together for the day. Your mom has already washed your clothes, I'll get you out to the stores just as soon as you have your strength back."

Hanna gasped, "Where are my clothes? They were all hanging in the guest house."

"Honey," Hanna's mom leaned down to her level, "You need to listen to Pete and Sam today. We are all here for you, remember that."

Sam pushed Hanna down the hall and into the dining room, "Good morning everyone!" All smiles awaited Hanna, except she wasn't smiling. She realized there was something very wrong. Hanna hardly ate anything for breakfast, she was anxious and bewildered. The past two weeks seemed to have never existed and for the life of her, she could not comprehend anything that was going on. Hanna felt lost, uncertain of her future, distant from the love she knew she had shared with Sam.

"I would like to go back to my room please."

Sam touched Hanna's hand as she pulled away, "Is everything ok?"

"I just want to go back to my room.

Sam wheeled her towards the elevator, he tried making small talk, however, Hanna was uninterested. He strolled her into her room and helped her into bed. "We were going to decorate your room today for the Christmas season. I loved your ideas and your mom and Mrs. Whittle loved them as well." Sam pulled out his stethoscope and arm cuff to take Hanna's blood pressure, he listened to her lungs and heart and examined her eyes, just to be sure of no swelling in the optic nerve. With the head trauma Hanna experienced It was mandatory for him to keep a close watch.

"Sam, what happened to me? Why can't I remember any of it and why was and am I still convinced that we were a couple?"

"I promise to answer all of your questions tonight when Pete is around, he was who saved you, I was the first person able to get to you." Sam looked deeply into Hanna's eyes, "Please don't worry beautiful, none of us are going anywhere." He kissed Hanna on the forehead and walked out of the room. Hanna's parents and the Whittles made their way up to see her with goodies in hand. Christmas tree, decorations, fresh Christmas blankets, candles, everything for Hanna to have a peaceful slumber.

"Knock knock my dear, we've all come to turn your room into your winter wonderland." She watched one by one enter with smiles on their faces. Sam walked in last, giving Hanna a wink and a smile carrying towels and the stockings that would hang from the mantle. Hanna smiled as she placed her hand over her face. Sam was flirting with her, she felt it in her soul. "So, we hear you have all the ideas on how to get this room ready for the Holidays! Hanna's mom sat in the winged back chair.

"Yes, Sam and I already spoke of..." Hanna stopped for a moment as if she was shaking a dizziness from her head. "Well umm, yes I know how I would like it for the future guests to enjoy." They all stood awaiting her instructions. "Oh, um, I thought about moving the television onto the fireplace mantel, that would free up the table that could be used on this side of the bed." Hanna pointing to how she would like things arranged. "Then we are left with the perfect spot for the tree. I thought about three wreaths with pinecones in the bay window with white ribbon, I think white needs to be the theme in here. But they can't be hung too low, the pictures one can paint from sitting in this chair as they watch winters wonder are glorious. And another in the window next to the fireplace and oh one more in the bathroom window."

"Sam, do you have enough wreaths for all of this?" Mrs. Whittle snickering as she was unwinding the strands of lights.

The fireplace held a long strand of liberty pine garland with pinecones that dangled along the mantle shelf, there were crystal candle holders of all shapes and sizes that boost white shimmering candles of assorted sizes. Sam hung three white stockings, one with an H, another with a C and the last with an S. Hanna's eyes filled with tears as she watched the last stocking hung. "Well you were right," Sam looking over to Hanna with a wink. "The television fits perfectly in between the crystal candlesticks."

"See, this is what I had envisioned all along. Once the tree is finished it will give a welcoming glow along with the fireplace." Hanna wiped a falling tear from her cheek. Pete had gotten the tree up with all its magnificent branches fluffed and filled. Mr. Whittle was taking care of placing all the white lights upon the tree while Hanna's mom and Mrs. Whittle were plucking through the ornaments to hang just the crystal snowflakes and angels at Hanna's request. "Mom, where's dad?"

"Oh, he's fixing a couple of things that Sam needed help with in the kitchen, you know your father he's always fidgeting with something if it needs to be fixed." Hanna slipped a slight giggle as she sat up in bed watching the Lilac room transformed into a glistening snowy Christmas. It was elegant, not overdone, just enough to welcome guests for a hypnotic sleep.

"Hanna, I found this old antique mirror with a thick silver etched frame, thought it would look great over the bed, maybe with some of the pine garland stuff you used on the mantel."

"Garland stuff?" Hanna giggled out loud. "Pete that would almost be perfect, I love the idea, could we hand three or four white ornaments from the garland as well?" Sam helped Hanna up from the bed walking her over to the winged back chair. The snow was still breathtaking and as Hanna was finally able to see the room from now a different view, it had all come together just as she thought.

"The only thing missing dear is the Christmas pillows for the chairs and window seat, we will bring those up in just a bit. They were a little dusty, so I decided to dry wash them. Mr. and Mrs. Whittle got up to go check on the pillows, Hanna's mom had laid the ornaments out ready to be hung as she excused herself as well with Pete, leaving only Sam and Hanna together.

Sam struggled for words, for Hanna's beauty and demeanor had all but left him putty in her hands. "So beautiful, want to decorate your tree?"

"Would love to," Hanna expressed with delight. "One thing, the lamp on the other side of the bed is exquisite, do you have another one for this side of the bed?"

"Yes, it's in storage, it needs a new part for it to work, but maybe we could ask your dad for his assistance."

"Yes, of course, he would love to do it and it would add the final touch to the room." Sam sat Hanna into her wheelchair pushing her closer to the tree, he moved the side table over for her temporarily and filled it with ornaments that she would be able to reach. "Looks like we didn't have all that many angels and snowflakes but seems your mom and Mrs. Whittle found some beautiful woven glass balls that we can fill in empty spaces."

Hanna busy placing precisely the gems of yesterday upon the tree guided Sam as to where to place his. "There beautiful, this is by far the most charmed time of the year. The decorating, smells of yesterday filling the air, the clear night sky with its glistening stars and the snow." Hanna's eyes were lit up like a little girl getting ready for Santa. Sam found himself just staring at her in amazement. Was she the one? The one he had wished for so many times... He quickly shook off what seemed to be cold chills, reminiscing over the past loves whose lives he had ruined as he finished hanging the ornaments on the mid-section to the top of the tree." "Did your mom have any snowflake tree toppers or supplies to make things?" She saw sadness in Sam's eyes,

"Um what? I'm sorry..." Hanna trying to bounce him out of his trance.

"Tree toppers, snowflakes, hello!" Sam stood there for a moment, "I have four or five boxes of craft supplies and two snowflake toppers, they're kind of old and definitely could use a makeover." Sam went to the basement, dingy but filled with the past to retrieve the two snowflake ornaments his mom had. On his way back upstairs, he shook off the past to focus on the present. "What do you think of these?" One was stained glass in a 3-D image, beautiful and only needed some hot soapy water to clean it up, the other had been handmade, it was flocked pinecone and fern with a distressed snow look along with crystal beads that had been carefully placed, each nestled inside. Hanna immediately fell in love with this exquisite piece. Taking a cloth shining all the beads, she then fluffed out the fern.

"It's absolutely priceless, the most beautiful thing I've ever seen."

"So, I guess this is your choice for a topper?"

"Perfect," Hanna sighed, closing her eyes for a moment in pure contentment. She wheeled herself over next to the entry door looking at the whole room. Sam placed the topper upon the tree and plugged it in. He then lit each candle upon the mantel. "Sam, come over here. Look, the room is perfect, it's complete." Sam walked over to Hanna standing behind her as he bent over wrapping his arms around her from behind. As Sam stood there he felt he had overstepped the boundaries with he and Hanna. Not moving and stuck in the moment he felt Hanna's hand reach over his arms. Her touch was soft, warm, comforting. "Sam don't let me fall." Sam with a confused look upon his face didn't understand the meaning of what Hanna had just said, but if it was falling in love, he needed that help as well, for Hanna was everything that he could have ever imagine in one person. "Sam, these walls are filled with so much love and I'm not talking about right at this moment, I mean from the past." Sam's mom used to always say that

The Colonel still watched over everyone who entered. Hanna let out a yawn, "The little girl's voice of song is soothing to me and the little sailor boy, well, I think he loves the house being filled with so many people. It's reassuring to him that there are so many within the walls, within the home itself. I think the spirits feel at peace," Sam knew deep down that love still roamed the halls.

15
LOST IN THE MOMENT

It was a calm night, Hanna had decided to dine in her room, taking in all the magic that spoke to her from within. She sat at the window, staring out to the universe, making a wish as she had done as a little girl. There was always a calmness that covered her body by the enchantment that filled the night sky. Hanna gathered her thoughts, pulling the crochet blanket from the bed. She wrapped herself tightly in the robe that she recalled wearing often and slipped on a pair of socks. Steadily walking to her wheelchair, she enfolded herself comfortably, wheeling herself into the hall. On her way towards the elevator, she caught a slight glimpse of a lovely lady dressed in Victorian clothing floating up the staircase. Hanna gasped, not knowing if what she had just witnessed was a figment of her imagination or from the head trauma she had endured.

Taking a detour, she slipped up to the third floor knowing Pete and the Whittles were downstairs with her parents. Impatiently waiting for the elevator doors to open, she wheeled herself in. Hanna knew something wasn't right. It was a completely different world, dust thick to the lungs. There was a very disapproving feel in the air. With each door she opened sorrow filled Hanna's heart. Maybe only because at one time this floor once had a life of its own. But what she was seeing wasn't real. Pete's apartment, Mr. and Mrs. Whittle's new home, where was it all? It's as if no one had been up here in years. There was no lady dressed in Victorian, however, Hanna felt the presence maybe of maids or housekeepers. Whichever it was, she could feel pain, the hopelessness of knowing what once was, was simply gone. Hanna could not help but focus on the past era that drew her to this location. How it was and what it could be again.

With an uneasy feeling, Hanna scurried to the elevator. For the same outline and shape of a woman appeared again in front of her while awaiting the doors to open. She seemed to be looking directly into Hanna's eyes instead of through her. Hanna realized at that very moment that her gift had never been lost or taken away, it had been laying dormant to a world that had become stagnant.   Down the elevator and to the first floor she managed not to disturb anyone. She soon found herself out on the side porch taking in the crisp air where she continued to speak to the heavens.

Bathed by the glistening night sky she spoke of Sam, knowing in her soul that he was the one. She had dreamt often of this love that only seemed to exist during her unconscious state. But he was there, right in front of her. She sat soundlessly imagining a winter wedding. Autumn, bringing little feet running through the yard. Daisies, that when freshly picked covered a porcelain skinned little girls face with curly champagne blonde hair. She had big blue eyes, a smile that was contagious, her name, Emma. Hanna had lost track of time; a familiar voice spoke from behind.

"Hey ladybug, what are you doing out here?"

"Pete! just sitting here star gazing, I've been cooped up for so long it was nice to get out into the fresh air."

"Well, are you about done? It's cold out here, we don't need you getting sick."

"Only if you promise to tell me what happened to me... to us." Hanna studied Pete's eyes with such concern, she was lost, a part of her missing.

"Yes ladybug, I'll tell you everything, but first I want Sam in the room with us and I want you in bed and warmed up, no falling asleep this time. As I remember we tried this the other night."

"Deal, can you take me back up, I don't want to unwrap myself, I'm actually kind of cold. Hanna looked up at Pete who was standing behind her with that distressed look upon his face. "Don't be sad Pete, whatever horrific thing happened to us, we survived, we're still here."

Sam had excused himself from everyone in the gathering room to go visit with Hanna, as he started walking up the stairs he stumbled upon Pete and Hanna entering back in from the side door. "Everything all right Pete?"

"Oh yes, just caught our little ladybug outside star gazing is all, brought her in before she caught a death of a cold." Hanna looked up at Pete with a smile and hurt in her eyes. Sam got Hanna comfortable in her bed, Pete sat quietly in the window seat. You could tell that he had so much on his mind and wasn't sure where to start.

"Pete, come over here." Pete lifted himself up and walked slowly over to Hanna's side of the bed. "Sit," she patted her hand on the down filled mattress. Her hand reached slowly placing it on the right side of his aged yet masculine face. "Tell me" her soft-spoken voice was relaxing to him.

"Well ladybug, long story short, you are right about boarding the train, me asking you for your ticket. I checked on you a few times up until the conductor came across the speakers. You thought he spoke of stopping in a small town due to the storm, but truth is, he was trying to warn us to take precautions for a train wreck. I'm still unclear myself how it all took place. I've read about it in the papers and have seen the stories on the news but for us, it was a totally different experience, no one would ever get the story straight." Pete's head dropped, rubbing his forehead and over his eyes. Sam sat quietly beside Hanna on the bed, listening, taking it all in. "The conductor didn't even finish his statement Hanna before the train started rattling, giving in as it turned onto its right side. Sliding, hearing the screeching of metal, passengers screaming and every unmounted piece of luggage, laptops, phones, anything that wasn't connected, flying in slow motion. When I came to my knees I was a car in front of you, don't even know how it was still attached, but the glass had broken from the doors. I was able to climb through to find you submerging into the water."

Hanna looked at Pete with such disbelief, "Go on."

"Well, you were unconscious, I couldn't get you to respond to me, the train had gone inaudible as if everyone were sleeping. I saw blood coming from your head and immediately applied pressure with I believe your scarf. I tied it off to help with the blood loss and to be able to have a free arm to pull you up and out of the water the best I could. All of a sudden everyone was screaming, frightened and confused. My medical side kicked in and tried to calm everyone that I could, asking them to check themselves for any abnormalities or pain. But I could not let you go to check on them myself. I promised you at the beginning that I would not leave you and I was trying my hardest to keep you up, out of the water and safe within my arm."

Hanna spoke softly, "It was so cold outside, why do I remember getting into a cab, seeing the colorful lights that strung across the streets before making our way to the Inn?"

"Ladybug, those weren't Christmas lights and we sure didn't go to any Inn. The passengers who weren't hurt helped care for the ones that needed it the most. There was smoke, the smell of metal filled the cabin. None of us could reach the windows, even with many broken out. The snow was falling hard, so not only did I have the river water flowing into the train, we had the frigid air along with the snowfall to consider as well. No one knew each other but somehow, we managed to all end up in the same area of the cabin keeping the injured all together that could be moved along with those of us able to help. The lights of the helicopters, firetrucks and emergency response teams let of a glow of what you could say looked like Christmas lights." He brushed Hanna's hair away from her eyes. "But they weren't Christmas lights. I was screaming for help, medical staff and firefighters came through the roof, which at that moment was the left side of the train. I was yelling so loudly for someone to help my ladybug and that's when Sam entered our lives." Pete paused for a moment, gathering himself from the fear that overwhelmed his soul once again. "I'm leaving out a lot of what we went through, but you were out cold. Some of the passengers were worse than you, which I came to find out. But you were my concern, my reason for pushing through my own pain to save you."

"Your arm," Hanna reached to Pete's arm, "it was broken, the pain you must have been experiencing."

"The pain was nothing compared to losing you." Hanna looked up at Pete noticing tears forming in such strong eyes.

"It all makes sense, I remember looking out at the river, in which I was actually in it. I remember seeing the train tracks, I was so cold. I'm assuming at this point that I didn't walk to any cab, but was placed in the back of an ambulance? That the Christmas lights I saw was either Heaven waiting for me or at some point became lucid enough to notice the colors of rescue vehicles." Hanna sat there pondering for a moment. It defiantly justifies the pain in my head and the bruises on my body. But nothing is as I remember."

Sam scooted closer to Hanna wrapping his arm around her as her head cradled into his arm and up against his chest. Tears came to her eyes, "I can't understand how I feel like I've been a part of this place over the past month." She looked up at Sam. "I know things about this home, I know every inch of this place and its history without even seeing most of it. We made so many memories, all of us, minus my parents. We made plans for the future. I'm so confused, my whole life was coming together and now, I'm being told it never existed. I was happy, truly happy."

Hanna could not stop crying, all the love, contentment, dreams, everything was gone within a fifteen- minute conversation. Sam squeezed Hanna, Pete held her hand, "Were still here, all together, every one of us that are in your beautiful dreams or amazing visions, were all here, right now." Sam spoke softly, "Your dreams hold much love, maybe you were destined to have those dreams, maybe you know something that we all don't, but will in due time." This gave Hanna a little comfort as she snuggled herself deeply into Sam's arms. As Hanna drifted off to sleep her kind words were embedded inside the men's hearts as they sat quietly just listening.

"My visions have never been happy ones, but somehow God knew where we were meant to be, he put us together to make a life of love and contentment. He showed me a glimpse of what can be. I choose hope and faith over disbelief I choose all of you."

Sam and Pete were quiet, watching Hanna as she slept. "Pete, do you think she understands what actually happened?"

Pete stood from the bed as he walked over to the door. "Not sure, but she obviously either knows something we don't or she's holding on to her dreams." Pete lifting his head from focusing on the ground, "Nah, I don't believe half of what I just said. I don't believe for a second, it's a dream thing. She knows too much about the place, who moved in here, the history of the past family who's spirits still resided here. It's like we were all with her but in a past life so to speak. She mentioned many things of the land that justaren't visible here anymore. She knows exactly where things are, the hidden staircase, the old bowling alley in the basement for the love of God." Pete shaking his head as he rubbed his eyes with a shaky hand. "This girl is meant to be here, I don't know how and for what reason, but she belongs just like you and I do." Without saying anything else Pete walked out of the room pulling the door shut behind him. Sam was still dressed in his clothes from the day but didn't want to wake Hanna, he pulled the blanket from the bottom of the bed, situated the pillows behind his head, kissing Hanna on hers. "Good night beautiful."

Morning had come, there was an unidentified feeling in the air. The house was calm and quiet. Hanna was still asleep as Sam lay there in thought. "What if Pete was right, what if all of this happened for a sincere reason, not a fluke or by chance, but by real destiny. I have no explanation for anything she knows and feels, she's an absolute angel laying here in quiet slumber. I'm sure she has her moments where I will want to run, but she's everything I've wanted and yet I know nothing about her." Sam realized swiftly by the clock on the table that the reason for the silence was due to the fact that he was awake at least two hours before anyone would be up. An epiphany, possibly. Sam pulled one of the pillows more under his head, wrapping his arms tighter around Hanna as he drifted back off into slumber.

The house that had been asleep was alive. The smell of coffee filled the hallways and the warmth of laughter filled Sam's heart. He rolled over to say good morning to Hanna, but she wasn't there. "Hanna, Hanna, where are you?" He jumped to the door and down the stairs, but before he could say a word he found Hanna in the kitchen with everyone.

Hanna felt Sam's presence enter the room. "Good morning Sam, did you sleep well?" "Hanna, I didn't know where you were, I woke up this morning and you weren't there. I guess it startled me."

Mrs. Whittle was taking her sweet muffins out of the stove. "She's been down here with us for about an hour and someone has not put Cloe down since they laid eyes on each other this morning."

"I've missed her, she's sleeping with me tonight, I need that little nose breathing on me."

Sam with a worried look, "Oh no, no we have guests arriving today for Thanksgiving week, I need to get us moved over to the carriage house and get the Inn together."

"We do, and it's all been taken care of." Pete turned with his hot cup of coffee taking a seat at the kitchen table.

"But we need the Lilac room."

"Yes, yes we do. Hanna's dad has been busy with me this morning getting the carriage house set up for Hanna's wheelchair. We thought maybe since you had to be back at the hospital tomorrow we would get ladybug, her parents and most likely you ready for their new home. Mr. Callaghan came through the kitchen door. "Morning Sam... morning beautiful." He kissed Hanna gently upon the top of her head. "Pete told me all the cozy things that Hanna remembered of how the carriage house was set up, Pete and I have been up since the crack of dawn getting it all together. Even got the fireplace going for all of us."

"He looked down at Hanna, I'm sure it isn't exactly what you remember in those beautiful dreams of yours, but I must say with Sam living there and the little touches we added, I think it's going to be a delight. Sam, I hope you don't mind that we took the opportunity, you've been so busy taking care of our daughter, I just didn't want any more on your plate."

Sam smiled, "No, I appreciate all the help everyone has been giving me. Taking care of Hanna has been a pleasure. I know we must get Hanna moved but you all are more than welcome to stay in your room if you wish.

"No, no, the phone rang this morning, wanting to know if we had any more room here at the Inn and guess what? We do. We have all six rooms booked now and only need to get two clean, which the Mrs. has already started on ours. Pete and I have even moved all of our belongings over to the guest room of the carriage house."

"I can't believe this, you all are amazing. Wait, we have four rooms upstairs."

Mrs. Whittle spoke up, "Yes, but with the two rooms downstairs we were able to accommodate two more sets of guests bringing in the additional income from all of us being here."

Sam with a worried look on his face, "But I do need to go shopping, make sure we have all the food we need to take care of everyone."

"That's been taken care of," Mrs. Whittle speaking up." Mr. Whittle and Pete are going to the grocery this morning with the money you had set aside for the week's food. Hanna's mom and I are going to make ahead everything we need that can be refrigerated for the next two days with ease, leaving less to do each day. We also revamped the breakfast situation, even with so many of us, where not a complaint will be had."

"You're amazing," kissing Mrs. Whittle on the cheek, you all are amazing." Sam sat down at the kitchen table after pouring a cup of coffee with such relief in his eyes. Hanna's dad stood against the kitchen counter warming up his hands next to the stove.

"I started a nice fire in the gathering room, should keep going for three or four hours while we give the finishing touches to this place before everyone starts arriving. We can get Hanna adjusted across the way and then her mom will join me at the grocer, so we can stock your fridge and cabinets."

"What for? I can't have you all spending your money. I can run out."

"Nonsense," Hanna's mom tapping Sam on the shoulder.

"You have been more than generous sharing your home with us, feeding us, taking care of our Hanna along with seeing that we all have had what we needed. It's the least we could do, along with lending a helping hand tonight at check-in. I've always wanted to work at an Inn, I know how to handle reservations and Pete and Mr. Callaghan, excuse me, George,"

Mrs. Callaghan rolling her eyes at her husband. "They are more than willing to be the bellhops for the evening, getting everyone situated in their rooms while Mr. and Mrs. Whittle work on dinner. You're covered, we have it all under control so that you and Hanna can get familiar with the guests. I'll be up in the morning and will come over to help with breakfast prep, it's all going to be perfect."

Sam just sat in sincere shock, "I never could have ever asked for a more loving family this holiday season, all of you have done so much more than I ever could have anticipated, all of the rooms are decorated, the whole Inn is decorated, it's beautiful and filled with so much love. Words will never be able to express my gratitude." He looked down at his coffee cup without another word as everyone looked away from him.

Hanna slipped her hand under the table grabbing on to Sam's hand. "You never let me fall, we're not about to let you." Sam squeezed her hand, eyes filled with tears, his heart overcome with adrenaline and warmth.

Christmas in Hunter's Grove

16
OPEN HANDED

The Inn along with the snow-covered grounds were picturesque. Gas lanterns illuminated the walkway up to the porch to the 1800's beveled mahogany glass doors. Every Christmas tree was set alight with each fireplace ignited. A soft glow from the gas lanterns that streamed the grand staircase was the finishing touch. Hanna and Sam greeted each guest as if they were longtime friends as Hanna's mom checked them in one by one. Mrs. Whittle was sure to walk everyone up the staircase to their suites, where the glow of the gas lanterns guided them with every step. As it was one of the Inn's most magnificent masterpieces.

Pete and Mr. Callaghan taking care of the luggage took their time as the guests were shown to their private suites, allowing them to get acquainted with their surroundings. Everything was going even better than planned.

Sam and Hanna were the first to make their way back down to the gathering room. Her first night of taking in the scenery that in her dreams she had come to love so much. "Everything is perfect Sam, we all did it." Hanna took it easy walking over to the couch where she pulled herself up from her wheelchair, sitting on the corner with her legs up by her side. "Do you think it would be ok if I had a glass of wine with everyone tonight?"

Sam walked over sitting beside her, "Sweet white? Let me guess."

"Hanna turned her head towards Sam, how did you know?"

"Easy ladybug, I know you get heartburn, well red wine is a no-no and I found two bottles of Dolce White mixed in with the groceries. I wondered how they got there?"

266

Hanna smiled with a soothing laugh, "Well it could have been for the guests or my mom you know. But you guessed right. I love sweet reds, but yes heartburn can be a bit of a pain, the white is smoother, crisper to the taste buds."

"In my dreams, we always sat by this very fireplace. I always had a glass of white in my hand and you with a bourbon. Not much of a drinker, nor am I. Just a nice place to simply take in the moments of the day that lead to a beautiful evening." Sam loved listening to Hanna as she spoke of her dreams, nothing that she ever said could not have been the truth. Sam knew in his heart all her stories were real, he just didn't know how.

The guests had started accumulating in the dining room. Sam and Hanna slipped quietly into the kitchen to help Mrs. Whittle and Hanna's mom put the finishing touches on dinner while Pete was setting the table for ten. Every glass filled with raspberry water topped off with raspberry mint ice cubes. The beverage table had been finished with the drink of the night being Mrs. Whittles caramel coffee hot chocolate with a dash of Baileys. Everyone was seated and introduced to each other and left to enjoy their first course of a Grapefruit, Endive, and Arugula Salad. The main course was delivered soon after offering Cornish Hen, Salmon, Rice Pilaf, and a Roll. An open bar of coffees, wine and sodas for the guest's likings.

Finally, Mrs. Whittle's sweet confection of mini pumpkin cheesecake trifles. The guests enjoyed themselves immensely. Two and a half hours later the stories that filled the evening had ended. Bellies were full and instead of most settling into the gathering room for a nightcap, they bid everyone a good night with a smile on their face and coffee in hand.

One by one, the doors closed at the Inn. Mrs. Whittle, Mrs. Callaghan and Hanna washed the dishes, putting away the leftovers in the fridge, as the men brought everything into the kitchen cleaning up the dining room. The breakfast menu was ready to go for the morning and everyone with such a long day behind them, were ready to turn in with the rest of the guests.

Before that happened Sam had caught the attention of Pete and Mr. Callaghan to join him for a few moments in the dining room. "Mr. Callaghan, I asked Pete to join us for a few moments because frankly sir, I'm a nervous wreck."

Mr. Callaghan looked across the table to Pete and then to Sam. "Well, I hope there isn't something wrong with my Hanna!"

"Oh, no sir, actually quite the opposite." Pete stepped in seeing that Sam was struggling with his words.

"I've only known your daughter for a couple of weeks and took care of her for a couple more, everything I ever heard from Pete about Hanna in their short time together and then my time with her. Seeing her around you and her mother, how she has made major improvement. Sir, I've fallen in love with your daughter and it becomes stronger with each passing day. I know you're going to tell me it's too soon, but Hanna is crazy, full of love, full of life, she's stubborn and apologetic all at the same time. She can laugh and cry in the same day and then laugh some more. I want to spend the rest of my life getting to know her quirks, what makes her tick and be the reason she smiles at least once a day. What I'm trying to say is... " Sam took a long breath and held it for a moment. "I would love nothing more than to have your approval. I would like to ask Hanna to marry me." Everyone sat quietly for a moment at the table.

"Damn boy, who am I to say no. I knew Hanna's mom was the one for me after a week of dating her. When you know you just know? Of course, you have my blessing."

Sam with a sigh of relief, "It won't happen tonight or this week. I have something up my sleeve where I want things to be as perfect as they can be. Sir, I promise with my heart I will take care of her with my whole being."

As they walked back into the kitchen in light conversation they saw that Mr. and Mrs. Whittle had retired up to their new suite for the evening. "Lord it's gotten late." Pete letting out a yawn.

Hanna squinting her face, "Late, it's 8:15, lightweight tonight Pete?" Snickering under her breath.

"No ma'am ladybug, I just think it's time for a nice hot shower and a bit of television with a hot cup of coffee before turning in for the night. Tomorrow morning brings hungry guests." He gave her a hug and a kiss upon her forehead and bid good night to the rest of the family before settling in for the evening.

Sam, Hanna and her parents prepared themselves for the walk over to the carriage house. It had once again become bitter cold with the temperatures dropping quickly. Hanna grabbed Cloe tucking her deep inside of her coat. Making their way along the sidewalk Hanna's mom had stated that they were going to head to bed as well. "Breakfast will come early, and I want to be sure to be over to help the Whittles in the morning. Would not want such a task to be on their shoulders alone."

Sam spoke softly as he opened the door. "No worries, I believe we are going to do the same thing. I have to be up for work and we can't operate a B&B

270

without all-hands-on-deck." Everyone had settled in, as they had fallen asleep swiftly. Hanna took out her journal and sat in the window seat as she stared out over the landscaped yard.

"Night has fallen quickly upon us this cold winters night; however, the glimmer of the snow is giving off a soft candlelight affect across the grounds. Just enough to help those who may be lost in thought find their way. I sit here tonight gazing at Sam and Cloe as they sleep in quiet slumber. I realized how blessed I am all due to a train wreck that turned my life into pure enchantment. I'll never quite understand how The Inn and its bygone era drew me to a life I had not lived. The only explanation, the old Colonel himself had a hand in uniting Sam and me as an unexpected gift. I miss the lilac room for it is where I felt the presence of the Old Colonel checking in on me from time to time, the whisper of the maids passing through and where I first fell asleep in Sam's arms. I may have been given the gift to know the past here at the Inn, but I look forward to life unfolding within the walls and the grounds as years pass. For a charmed love will only pass through your life once in a lifetime."

Hanna settled in for the night, drifting off as she curled up against Sam. For tonight had brought great comfort to Hanna. She was where she belonged with the man from her dreams.

Morning came quickly with the aroma of coffee lingering throughout the carriage house Hanna was the last one to awaken, for sleeping in ease had not come easy. She finally made it over to the Inn just in time to help serve breakfast to the guests.

"Good morning ladybug sleep well?"

"Yes, I can't even remember dozing off." "Well, Sam must have been up at the crack of dawn this morning. I came down to get my coffee and found that the dining room had already been set up with this note for you."

Good Morning Sunshine,
I'll be home around seven thirty tonight, have yourself together. I have something amazing to show you. Make sure to dress warm. Don't need you catching a cold.
Love Sam

Hanna spent most of the morning like a lost puppy dog, wondering what Sam could be up to. Breakfast could have not gone more perfect and for the guests, they were a delight. Hanna took it upon herself to check each door to see if anyone wanted service for the day on their rooms. With each passing door, "No Service" was the answer. Hanna took the elevator down to the first floor where she caught up with Pete. "Well, no one needs anything in their rooms, so I guess I'll go ahead and just straighten up down here."

"Not much to do ladybug and with you just starting to walk, what overnight, without your wheelchair, you need to take it easy."

"Yeah, I'm a little winded this morning but I haven't felt more alive." Pete and Hanna slowly walked into the dining room making sure everything would be perfect for tomorrow morning's breakfast. Dinner was only served one day a week and on Saturday nights, so it made it very welcoming to know there wasn't much to do. As always Mrs. Whittle was in the kitchen making more delightful confections for the evenings. Her mom had wiped down everything in the dining room and entry area with Mr. Whittle helping the Mrs. out with the dishes. "How is everyone this morning?" Hanna peeking into the kitchen with a bright smile upon her face.

"Look at you, where is your wheelchair?" Hanna's mom walking over to her with a welcoming hug.

"Trying not to use it since Sam isn't around today. Figured I can't get yelled at too much." Hanna letting out a soft laugh.

"Well, we have a plate of leftovers for you in the microwave if you're hungry?"

"I'm famished," opening the microwave door to see what surprise was in store.

"I'm going to go ahead and make my cranberry muffins for tomorrow morning and Mrs. Whittle is working on her famous sugar cookies and snickerdoodles for our guests tonight. Do you have any idea what you would like for dinner tonight?"

Hanna's mom turned as she took Hanna's breakfast from the microwave. "Nope, Sam left a note for me to be ready at seven thirty, he's taking me somewhere and told me to dress warm. I'll help, why don't we just make Mrs. Whittle's garlic chicken noodle soup along with double grilled cheese sandwiches tonight? Simple, yet perfect for a cold night."

Mrs. Whittle turned around with a perplexed look upon her face. She started to ask Hanna how she knew about her soup when Pete quickly called her attention to the hall. "Mrs. Whittle remember, Hanna isn't like us, she is recalling either things that Sam and I spoke of at the hospital or somehow she just knows."

"I forgot, I've never met anyone like Hanna before and frankly it's hard to understand something that I know nothing about. Not everyone needs to know, some won't accept her. You know how mean people can be."

"I do, so when she spouts off like that, we need to just look normal. Sam and I can handle it later if need be reminding her that she either wasn't there or finding out how she knew."

Mrs. Whittle gave Pete a wink as she popped back into the kitchen. "So, my dear what exactly are you doing tonight with Sam?" Mrs. Whittle sitting down to enjoy a cup of coffee with Hanna's parents.

"I really don't know, he just told me to dress warm and to be ready at seven thirty tonight. I hate the cold, I really hope we aren't going to be hanging around outside, I'm freezing just thinking about it." Hanna's face filled with color, eyes as bright as the sky. The work had been done for the day besides just keeping an eye on the Inn. Everyone had retired to their new homes for the day. Hanna took it upon herself to explore every inch of the Inn on her own starting with the basement. It was dark, dreary, heaviness filled the air. With each turn, she came upon years of history until she came to what used to be the old bowling alley. Nothing was really left; the lanes were barely noticeable, but Hanna could see the beauty that laid within. She climbed back up the stairs taking a moment to catch her breath before deciding to head into the kitchen to brew a pot of coffee. It had bothered her greatly what she had seen on the top floor. She knew that it held a living area of its own along with two apartments now for the Whittles and Pete, but what she witnessed the other night she needed to see for herself what it looked like. Entering the elevator, she closed her eyes as it eased its way to the top, doors opening slowly. Peeking out of one eye, it was clean. No dust in the air and a glimmer of the sun shined through the windows. She knew they both had their own kitchens, but with her brain working the way it had been lately she knew she could get away with saying she had forgot as she knocked on each door.

"Pete are you awake?"

"Come in ladybug, she heard echo from the other side of the door."

"Thought you might want some coffee?" A fake smile upon Hanna's face.

"Coffee, you know I have a full kitchen, everything ok?"

"Yeah, just wanted to see what your place looked like. I came up here the other night after seeing I guess what appeared to be a ghost." Hanna sat down on the leather sofa, feeling it with her hands. Looking up at Pete, "This room is exactly what I saw in my dreams. Well maybe not the curtains, but it's everything I remember. It's not new to me at all." Hanna with tears in her eyes made eye contact with everything she had remembered, from the tall masculine beams on the ceiling to the openness where the hardwoods seemed to go on for miles.

"Ladybug, focus, what were you saying?" I came up here the other night. It was dark, hard to breathe from the dust in the air. None of this existed. I opened each door, at least six to find old abandoned rooms without life. I wasn't sure what I would find today. I know you have a kitchen, it was just my way of having an excuse to come up here."

"Well you never need an excuse, I'm glad you did come up. As you can see it's far from abandoned, it's actually full of life now and you my dear, I love hearing your stories." Hanna smiled getting up from the couch.

"I'm going to go back downstairs now, make sure there are no calls that came in. Mrs. Whittle said five thirty for dinner right?"

"Right, I'll be down in a bit, right now I'm enjoying my new home. So much better than my stuffy apartment. Still can't believe this is all happening."

"Well it is, and I love you." Hanna walked out of Pete's quarters pushing the button on the elevator.

Hanna had kept busy most of the day investigating the Inn. She had come across a couple of old books that held pictures of what the Inn once looked like compared to now. She sat behind the check-in counter mesmerized by the photos. Knowing she had been a part of the past somehow as with each passing picture there was something familiar about them. The guests seem to come and go throughout the day. The gathering room at times filled with laughter and general conversation.

Night came quickly with a familiar voice in the distance. "Hanna dear, are you going to join us for dinner?" Her mom peeked around the corner to find her daughter engulfed in pictures.

"Hey mama, yes, are we in the kitchen tonight?"

"Yes, why don't you put away those books, dinner is gonna get cold." Hanna and her mom walked in conversation of what she had explored during the day. Everyone was sitting around the table when she and her mom arrived.

"Have a good day today Hanna?" Pete looking up from his bowl.

"Yes, and I've lost track of time. Sam will be here in a couple of hours and I haven't even thought about getting ready. Pete, would you mind filling in for me at the front desk for the next couple of hours? I'll return the favor tomorrow."

"Of course, not like I won't be awake, I haven't rested like I did today in what seems forever. I don't think I've been this comfortable in a long time." Hanna scarfed down her dinner while halfway listening to the dinnertime conversation. She got up from the table washing her dishes by hand, filling everyone's glasses with what they were drinking before excusing herself.

Hanna had spent the last hour getting ready for her night out with Sam. Her stomach was in knots, but why. She had awakened to him every morning for the past couple of weeks and had fallen asleep each night within his arms. They had gotten to know each other's daily routines. She, however, knowing him a lot longer from her dreams. But with every breath he spoke to her, it felt like the first time, with each action or word she fell deeper in love. To Sam, he would never know her true thoughts. Each day was a new day of just living life with Hanna.

Hanna had laid Cloe down on her pillow by the fireplace while she put on her coat, hat and her mother's scarf. Picking Cloe back up she walked carefully over to the Inn. "Mom! I didn't know you all were still going to be in the kitchen."

Handing Cloe to Mrs. Whittle. "Why yes, you didn't think we were going to miss your first official date out with Sam did you?"

"Well, not our first," Hanna speaking quickly and remembering even quicker than what she had said never took place. Hanna turned around after filling a thermos with Mrs. Whittles coffee/ hot chocolate confection. Do I look all right?" Pete stood from the table, each hand on Hanna's shoulders.

"You look perfect ladybug." Hanna smiled as she grabbed two disposable coffee cups from the Inns' cabinet.

The doorbell rang before Hanna could sit down at the table. Everyone got up from their seats, knowing it was Sam. They followed behind Hanna to the front entrance. Hanna opened the door to find Sam standing there with a single white rose and a horse-drawn sleigh outside of the Inn. "What in the world?" Hanna gasped.

"I have something to show you, I promise you won't be disappointed." Hanna decided to not say a word, for the smile upon her face spoke a thousand. He helped her into the sleigh covering both with a heated blanket as he sat beside her. The ride was delightful. The snow glistened, danced and twirled upon the streets, trees and buildings. The lights that strung across Main Street added to the dream effect that Hanna was having. There was no way possible that something so beautiful existed. She heard music in the distance. The sleigh stopped right in front of the courthouse. It was lit in the most beautiful of colors of blues, greens, reds, purples and pinks that danced with every beat of the music. The trees on the grounds were decorated in the same vibrant colors, mannequins lined the walkway. It was the most exquisite site Hanna had ever laid her eyes upon, besides the man of her dreams who stood in front of her.

"Sam, this is the most perfect moment of my life." Hanna's hand gripped Sam's as they walked up to the benches where he had already laid a blanket upon the front left side just for them. "How did you get all of this done? You've managed to turn Christmas, well, magical for me again just like as a little girl seeing Santa for the first time. Sam helped Hanna sit on the bench, covering her with the blanket from the sleigh.

He handed Hanna a red envelope. "Open it."
Sam standing in front of her. With her eyes full of
questions, she did as he asked.

I've known you for a month, taken care of you
for two but have dreamt of you for a lifetime. I can't
and don't want to imagine life without you for a single
moment. I want to grow with you, learn our quirks
and what brings sparks to your eyes. I want you now
and for the rest of my life."

He knelt before her, pulling his mother's
antique emerald shaped wedding ring from his
pocket. "

Make me the happiest man alive, be mine from
this moment on. I promise to make you smile every
day and kiss any tears away that may form in those
beautiful green eyes. I promise I'll always be here, I'm
not going anywhere. Marry me, Hanna."

"Yes, oh my goodness yes, are you sure,
really?" Sam laughing with tears falling from his eyes,
yes, I'm sure. I could not be surer. Hanna stood with
tears streaming down her face as she leaned in to hug
Sam. They stood there swaying to the melodies that
echoed across the town. Hanna had her perfect
moment in time. The one she would tell her children
and grandchildren about one day. For she had found

the love of her life by chance in a little town known as Hunters Grove.

Christmas in Hunter's Grove

17
Six Words

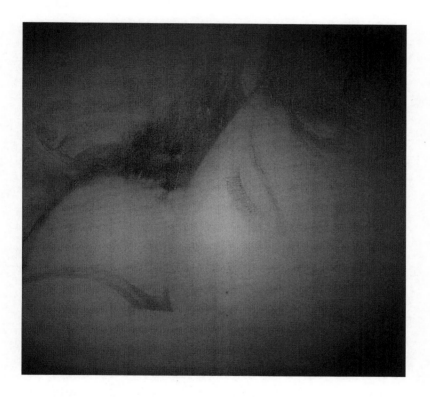

The next few weeks flew by. They all enjoyed making arrangements for flowers, the wedding cake and dress to running the Inn normally on a day to day basis. Hanna's recovery had been remarkable but still had not come to terms with the fact that she could not remember the crash. Hanna was able to spend time with her mom and dad going over the finest of details for a small family wedding. She didn't want tons of people from Sam's work, just the ones who meant the most to him. There would be no flower girl or ring bearer, no bridesmaids, only a groomsman and Cloe.

The day had come. The Inn was completely decorated for a beautiful Christmas ceremony. There wasn't much to do, for it was already seamless just the way it was. The food was prepped and laid out eloquently in the dining room. The gathering room carried the wedding cake along with the champagne and the three-piece quartet. The cake was a small three tier masterpiece made up of red velvet and white buttercream icing. The design, simple yet elegant complimented the décor. It flowed like the grand staircase. White roses and white camellias bloomed from the bottom. Pine sprigs and sugar-coated cranberries wrapped around the cake for an unflawed design. The topper was a blown glass ornament from one of the shops downtown in the shape of a rose with two hearts entwined. Hanna had accomplished getting the wedding gown on while keeping her hair and makeup intact. It was a sweetheart off the shoulder ball gown with a court train. The dress made of tulle and lace that flowed all around her. Hanna's dream dress thanks to Mrs. Whittle.

The moment had come. Hanna glided down the grand staircase to the soft melody of the music. Her father waiting at the bottom of the staircase to walk her through the entry of the gathering room. Hand in hand at the altar, Hanna's heart was full. She had imagined this day only in her dreams for many years. However, she could tell something was off, something wasn't quite right.

Sam had become jittery and unsure. Every relationship that had ever ended had entered his mind believing in his heart that Hanna was the cause of his past washing over him. Hanna stood there with tears forming as Sam looked into her eyes, touching her porcelain skin with the back of his hand. "I just can't do this anymore, you're all I ever dreamt about but I'm still dealing with my own demons. I know I love you, I know that I'm in love with you, but I haven't been truly happy in a long time and need to take care of me."

Hanna was trying to gather her words. "I don't understand, what has changed? We are perfect together. You're my rock, my crazy, my love filled with laughter and tears."

Sam's hand dropped from hers, he walked away never looking back. Hanna collapsed on to the floor, her anxiety and panic attacks became tenfold in an instant, a fallen angel. Hanna's mom and dad stood there in shock the same as the other guests. Pete quickly ran to Hanna kneeling onto the ground, slightly lifting her while he cradled her in his arms. Her tears fell as fierce as a broken damn, strong and fast making it impossible to see much less breathe. "Pete, what did I do? What have I done so wrong that he would just leave me?" Pete had no answers as he looked up at Janice, the only one who seemed to have known Sam the longest.

"I don't know ladybug, but I sure as hell plan on finding out."

Pete had helped Hanna up to his apartment for the night, her parents stayed behind with the others to rid the Inn of all memories of a wedding. "I don't understand why he would do this to my little girl." Hanna's mom cried the whole time as she rolled the twinkle lights. Janice finally spoke up,

"I know he had a couple of bad relationships where he had told me and others that the women had cheated on him and before Hanna there was Carol. They were together for about six years before they started falling apart. He believed she was cheating on him as well but never had the proof. Hanna obviously did something to snap back all of those memories convincing him that Hanna would do the same."

Mrs. Whittle could not help to add a bit to the conversation. Walking around the Christmas tree placing each glass heart and angel into their boxes, "He's never been the same since his parents passed away. He has a sister that hasn't been around in three years since she left for college. That about tore him apart completely. They didn't see each other a lot, but when she left, and he finally turned her room into a guest room it was as if he went through the empty nester syndrome. We all knew Carol, but to see them together you could tell that they just weren't destined to be. I think he just didn't want to be alone. But Hanna, I could have never imagined this happening. They were so happy just last week. Their plans for a honeymoon, oh my heart just hurts right now. I pray he postpones that trip and doesn't go with what should have been... " Mrs. Whittle could not manage to finish her sentence. The pain had not only hit Hanna but everyone within the Inn.

Pete left Hanna laying on the couch to make them both some coffee. All was quiet, no words or emotions were shown from her. Upon his return he found her laying on the ground with her cheek flush with the wood floor curled up in a ball. Hanna sweetie, why don't you let me get you some comfortable clothes and go lay in my bed. Her eyes never moved, nor did any part of her body, it was as if she went into a paralyzed state. He left her for a moment to go down to the Lilac room where she had used it this day for her wedding to collect her medications. Pete's phone had gone off four separate times with messages, but at that moment he was so worried about his little ladybug that he only glanced at it before placing it back into his pocket.

Upon his return, Hanna's head was lying in a puddle of tears. "Why Pete, he's the absolute love of my life, why?" Hanna's words were hard to make out for at times she was fighting for air. But the pain that showered throughout her whole body told the true story of just how much pain she was in. Her eyes were wide open again and the tears had stopped, however, her body still lay there lifeless.

"Hanna, I need you to take your medicine for me, can you do that?" Without even a glimpse up at Pete or at the medicine itself, she opened her mouth allowing him to place it under her tongue. "Pete how am I supposed to go on knowing the only man I ever truly loved left me, it's like a horrific death to my soul. How did this happen?"

Pete sat them quietly with Hanna, "Ladybug, please get up off the floor, go lay in my bed where you will be comfortable, please." He begged her once again.

"No, laying on the floor is allowing me to feel my heart beat, reminding me that this isn't a dream, that even though I'm alive I'm dead inside."

Pete could not help but wipe the warm, wet tears away from his own face with the back of his hand. The pain she was experiencing was going to slam against her harder over the weeks ahead. Right now, he knew she was in shock. It was now around midnight and she had finally drifted off to sleep. He laid a quilt upon her and pulled out his phone to see four messages. One from her father where he quickly sent a return message. "Mr. Callaghan, Hanna has finally fallen asleep, she ended up placing herself onto the floor refusing to get up. I've made sure that she has had her medicine and covered her with a quilt. I'll be sleeping on the couch tonight in case she is to wake. You and the Mrs. try and get some sleep tonight. Hopefully, we can make sense of this over the next few days."

He then went on to read the messages from Sam. "Pete, what did I do? How could I have listened to other people and not my own heart?"

The second message stated that Sam was staying in town at the local hotel away from work and the Inn. "Pete, I've made such a mess of things. I pushed away the only girl who ever loved me for me. I've had so much going on in my head and then taking care of Hanna at times well, I lost myself within the shuffle. I let my job consume me forgetting I had my crazy, my love and my in-between all along at home. I let my own self-get in the way."

Pete had not answered. He then went onto the third and final message. "Pete, are you there? Have I lost you as well? I need to make this right, I've done the unthinkable, blaming her, not giving her a chance to have a voice. Blaming her for things that I obviously blew out of proportion in my own head. I've done some unthinkable things to her all because of my own issues and selfish reasons. I love her, I'm in love with her, I just can't be with her right now. I've made too many wrongs, blaming her."

Pete had no words, nothing to respond with. Instead, he placed his phone in his pocket, grabbed a blanket off the recliner and laid on the couch to keep an eye on Hanna.

The sun was shining just enough to cascade through the clouds and through the window. Pete tried for over two hours to get Hanna up off the floor. He knew he needed help, something he was not able to offer at the moment. He went downstairs where he crossed paths with Hanna's dad as he was coming in from loading the car. Mrs. Callaghan sat in the kitchen with Mrs. Whittle discussing the situation at hand.

Mr. Callaghan turned, "How's my daughter doing this morning?"

"Pete looked at the floor and then up at him, "Not so good, I was coming down to get you. Thought maybe you could help me get Hanna up off the floor."

Mr. Callaghan was overwhelmed with grief. "You've never called her by her name before, why the sudden change?"

Pete's face blank from all the confusion, "Not sure, I'm feeling the devastation from Hanna's heart, I can't help her this time and I'm so angry I can't bear to stay here with Sam now. How do you destroy another's soul? How do you just walk away in the most cowardly of ways with no hesitation? That girl is in complete shambles." Pete stopped talking as the overwhelming feeling of guilt swept over his body and for no fault of his own.

It was around noon when Hanna lifted herself from the oak floor. Her mother had left a change of clothes on the armrest of the couch. Hanna stumbled to the bathroom. Her wedding dress had a v-cut Victorian buttoned back that she had made an effort to unbutton. In a matter of moments, she was screaming in agony ripping off the eloquent handcrafted gown that had been made just for her.

"I'm stuck," gasping for air as if she was being strangled. "Pete help, I can't do this, I just can't do this." He opened the door slowly.

"Ladybug it's me. Here let me help you." He walked in to find Hanna in a state of confusion. "Why won't it come off, it won't come off." Hanna was screaming with uncountable tears that rolled into one another as they dripped from her face. "Hanna, look at me, breathe!"

Pete with one hand on each shoulder had to be a little forceful to get Hanna to cooperate. "Sweetie just turn around, ok, let me help." Pete unbuttoned her dress so that she could slip off the top part of the dress. "Lift your arms," Pete guided her shirt over her head and arms pulling it down under the dress. "Now, slip on your leggings and once you're done we will get you out of the rest of this thing." Hanna turned to Pete, "I can't do this without you, I'm lost Pete, I'm truly lost."

As Hanna and her parents said their goodbyes to the Whittles, Pete spoke up asking Mr. Callaghan if he could make room for one more. Hanna turned to Pete, "You're coming with us?"

"If it's ok with your parents, I'll find my own little place, just may need somewhere to stay for a couple weeks or so." Mr. Callaghan was unsure of this arrangement, but he knew how fond his little girl had taken to Pete and really didn't want to cause her any more pain.

"Sure Pete, I can make some room in the trunk for your things." Pete scurried up the elevator, packing his clothes, he would come back another time to gather the rest of his belongings, as for now, he just wanted to be with Hanna.

The drive was long and unwelcoming, Hanna had left behind her home to live with her parents. No words were really spoken on the five-hour drive until they hit her parent's town.

"Imagine that", Pete spoke calmly.

"What do you mean? Hanna lifted her head from his shoulder.

"You never told me where you were from, I had no idea it would be this magnificent place." Hanna laid her head back down onto Pete's shoulder, "It's been at least fifteen years since I've lived here. I'm sure much hasn't changed and frankly I never really called this home. Something was always missing."

Two months had gone by, winter still in the air. Everyone was managing to move on from the blow to Hanna, except for Hanna herself.

"It feels as if it's been months since I picked up my journal. I still find myself sending letters every week with no response. Although it slashes me apart, I can never let him feel that he is not loved.

Everything that used to make me happy now sends rushing waves of tears down my face that fall into a lake surrounding me. I fight to breathe, crying so uncontrollably that my body shakes, pushing myself to gulp in air. My chest heavy and lungs filled with concrete, I fight every day just to exist. Six words that would forever change my life as I once knew it. Six words that broke my soul forever, "I just can't do it anymore."

My one true love disappeared as fast as he appeared within my life. It's as if he took a nail and hammered it through the center of my heart. But that's not the end, the nail is ripped out and swung into it again and again leaving so many painful holes and shredding my soul. I wish it would just explode taking me out of this horrific nightmare and suffering. No matter how much I try every day to wake with a smile, I find it's just too much to bear. I sleep most of the day, no energy, no appetite. I just stare out the window in silence and scream in my dreams. For the radiant beauty of the grounds along with the whimsical night sky has now turned dark. The things that once brought warmth to my soul and a smile to my heart I can do no more. I no longer listen to music, afraid a song will come on that will leave my body numb. I can't bring myself to go hiking in the mountains or floating under a waterfall with my friends, for with every step taken would be a reminder of him by my side. My world changed, I've become a bitter human being, trusting nothing and allowing no one to ever become close to me again. I do however pray for him each night. I'll never understand why we just could not communicate, why it had to be done in the most cowardly of ways. A true love isn't supposed to wilt or fade. It blooms, dropping petals along the way for the other to nurture and take care of until one day it becomes so strong that not a single petal will ever fall again. He promised to never leave me, he promised to love me always. I miss my best friend, I miss the love of my life. I will never not see him in my dreams, I will never stop loving the man who gave me back my life."

Hanna was trying eagerly to cope with the loss of her best friend and love of her life. She tried so hard, every day, to have a point of getting out of bed. Why were her days of laughter and love ripped away? How did the joy that once filled her life become such a deep depression? In a moment, a single moment it was just gone. Of course, she had heard the horror stories from others that knew Sam. It allowed Hanna's letters to slow down, until she was able to let go. Days of depression seemed to be happening more often. Then again, there were more days arriving with a smile than any day of sadness. But after all this time, Hanna still could not wrap her head around the fact that they weren't happy. No signs, nothing out of line, nothing ever added up. She still longed for his warmth and craved his touch. With questions left unanswered, Hanna would walk through life unwilling to ever love again, for what she had, was an undying love.

ABOUT THE AUTHOR

Kimberly was born in Silver Spring Maryland. Her parents gave her a great life growing up both on the east coast surrounded by Mountains and Seaside along with a short move to the Midwest country life. She is not only a water baby by nature but also considers herself attached to the earth, for Nature calms her spirit on hectic days. She currently resides on the East Coast with her family and dear friends.

Kimberly, a single mother most of her life was a well-known and successful Associate Broker for an Annapolis, Maryland Real Estate Firm for over 10 years. However, life changed and with the bad comes the good. She's a survivor of PTSD, Panic Disorder and

Anxiety disorder, although it can set her back at times, she pushes forward always learning new things. An empath from birth, she chooses to surround herself with the positive. Kimberly holds certifications in Graphic Design, Wedding Consulting, Floral Design and First Responder. She has coordinated numerous fundraisers on a large scale to help support local communities, children with cancer and speaking events. Still today she speaks of the hard work from the volunteers and that some things just can't be done alone.

Her current plans involve returning to the world of Real Estate, helping other fulfill their dreams, while working on her second book in the Forever Hanna Series. Kimberly looks at life as a gift. She's constantly learning and experiencing new things.

Made in the USA
Middletown, DE
14 December 2018